MITSY MORTE:
AFTERLIFE ATTORNEY

Playwright & Illustrator: Bob Clark

Brave Brothers Books LLC
1389 W. 86th Street #186
Indianapolis, IN 46260
www.bravebrothersbooks.com

Mitsy Morte: Afterlife Attorney

Twitter@BraveBrosBooks

Editor: Cadie Krivoniak
Cover & Interior Design: Suzanne Parada

Library of Congress Control Number: 2023933241

Published April 2023 in the United States by
Brave Brothers Books, LLC
ISBN 13: 978-1-952099-02-1

Licensing Information
For schools wishing to purchase a license to publicly perform Mitsy Morte: Afterlife Attorney, please send an inquiry to bobclarksanse@gmail.com.

CONTENTS

CAST OF CHARACTERS
(in order of appearance)
Several roles may be played by the same actor as needed.

JOSEPH COFFIN, elected Grim Reaper - Joe Coffin is a flashy, loud and in-your-face politician, the kind you see come up in New York politics a lot. He probably should've been a game show host or something, but he got a taste for the public spotlight from taking on the job of District Reaper, a lawyer who can send souls to the afterlife and threaten eternal punishments, making him a very powerful figure.

FRANK STEIN, *66 Minutes* news journalist - Frank Stein (professional name) got into journalism after extensive home schooling (public schools not being an option for someone of his... conditions) and gained a great deal of respect for cracking a top secret code to reveal the involvement of extraterrestrials in the Iran-Contra Affair. He has a complicated relationship with his "father."

JOURNALIST 1

JOURNALIST 2

JOURNALIST 3

ARI WESTPHAL, Grim Reaper's Chief of Staff/Campaign Crisis Manager - originally hails from the Fae, where he worked for the Oberon Administration, and negotiated the King's divorce from Queen Titania. He was an early supporter of Joe Coffin, and has successfully represented him since his first campaign for District Reaper, though he has grown more and more disillusioned.

COURIER

MITSY MORTE, lawyer & lesser demon - Mitsy Morte is one of the most flamboyant and devil-may-care attorneys on the afterlife circuit. Originally hailing from the suburbs of the second circle (basically the Coney Island of the Underworld), Mitsy started out as an entertainment lawyer, negotiating "Crossroads Contracts" to sell souls in return for success. However, she always had a little bit of a conscience, so she snuck in Halo Clauses to let her clients slip into Heaven, so she's never made the big bucks herself.

LUPINA, Mitsy's assistant & werewolf - Lupina (not her real name) has been working as Mitsy's private investigator, officially designated as "assistant" for legal purposes, only very recently after she came into town looking for a job under shady circumstances. Being a werewolf, she's used to having to pull up roots and assume a new identity every so often to escape both angry mobs and bad breakups, oftentimes both. Allegedly she recently has spent time in both Tokyo and Chicago.

DIANA DEWEY, lawyer DC&H - The firm of Dewey, Cheatam, and Howe is one of the oldest and most respected - begrudgingly so - law firms in the afterlife circuit. Mitsy Morte once worked for DC&H and was even on the fast track for partnership before she betrayed them and split to form her own private firm. Dewey, Cheatam, and Howe never forgave her, and they have sought to put their heads together (literally so, if the rumors of them being telepaths are true) in order to get their revenge.

HOWARD HOWE, lawyer DC&H

KEVIN MEPHISTO, DC&H client

DAVID MARCATO, DC&H client

ASSOCIATE 1

CHESTER CHEATAM, lawyer at DC&H

DONNY NOSFERATU, vampire - Donny is a simple vampire, clued in but not terribly high up on the Vampire Mafia. Like a lot of vampires, he has a nostalgic love for long past time periods, but while most vampires have an affinity for the 1800s, Donny's into the 1970s. He'll never admit this, however, but he was actually born in the 1990s and never actually lived in the time period he's so obsessed by (this is far more common in the vampire community than anyone will admit).

DOORMAN, name is Billy, but is called Jimmy

66 Minutes **NEWSGIRL 1**

66 Minutes **NEWSGIRL 2**

MEDUSA "MADDIE" SINCLAIR, lawyer & gorgon

66 Minutes **PRODUCTION ASSISTANT 1**

66 Minutes **PRODUCTION ASSISTANT 2**

JOCELYN IMHOTEP, Citizens for Joe party chairwoman - Jocelyn Imhotep has been involved in Joe Coffin's political arrangements ever since he became serious about making the jump from District Reaper to higher office, and in her position she's managed a very successful campaign. Before then, however, her history is a blank. She claims to be descended from Egyptian mummies, but there's no documentation of her line in the hieroglyphic registry...

GLINDA, a witch and co-host of *Witch's Brew in the AM*

ELMYRA, a witch and co-host of *Witch's Brew in the AM*

OMELAS, a cat and co-host of *Witch's Brew in the AM* - *Witch's Brew in the AM* is one of the most popular morning shows in the Tri-State Area. All three of them started out as staffers on *66 Minutes* under Frank Stein, and even began *Witch's Brew* as a kind of politically-oriented morning show for people to drink coffee over. But then the ratings came in, and it turned out that Glinda and Elmyra are really morning people in a big way. Omelas still takes his job seriously, but he's currently negotiating his contract. (Note: character can be played by an actor in cat costume or by an actor operating a cat puppet.)

Witch's Brew in the AM **CAMERA PERSON**

Witch's Brew in the AM **PRODUCTION ASSISTANT 1**

Witch's Brew in the AM **PRODUCTION ASSISTANT 2**

ANGEL 1, member of the Halo Squad

ANGEL 2, member of the Halo Squad

CLARENCE ODDBODY, senior angel & member of the Halo Squad - The Heaven Security Agency, known largely to its critics as the "Halo Squad," exercises a great degree of power in the afterlife circuit, and its agents are accused of privacy invasion in their surveillance almost as often as the North Pole (see the "Elf on the Shelf" scandal). Little is known about Clarence Oddbody, senior agent of the HSA, except that he has been accused of violating various time-and-space ordinances, such as the Bedford Falls case. Everything else is top secret.

GUARD

HONORABLE JUDGE FIREBRAND ABERNATHY - Coming from the illustrious and wealthy Abernathy family, one of the first dragons to immigrate to the Americas, Judge Firebrand went into public service to show that he cared about more than just sitting on a pile of gold all day. Ever since he made the bench, however, he's seen an endless litany of petty divorce squabbles, rich CEOs looking to stay out of minimum security Purgatory, and so, so many parking tickets. It's a wonder he doesn't breathe fire and burn the whole courthouse down.

BLUE HAIR

BOW TIE

BIRD MASK

DOPPELGANGER - Noun. German, "Double Walker." A living double of a person, an apparition with the same appearance, and personality, of someone. Common in German folklore, nightmares, and a mysterious netherworldly dimension sometimes known as "The Red Room"...

MAGICIAN - Among the documented residents of the strange world between worlds known as "The Red Room" is the person known as "The Magician." The Red Room is often used by the HSA as a tool for enhanced interrogation of prisoners who are unwilling to confess their crimes, and it is the Magician's job to twist their minds until they are ready to divulge all their information. In other words, spill the beans or you lose your marbles.

SOUND TECHNICIAN

DEVIL - Not just ANY Devil— he's THE Devil, baby! The original, you might say!

ACT I

SCENE 1: Press Conference

A podium with a political seal styled after the Presidential eagle, but with a vulture instead, a sickle in its talons. Political banners and posters are tacked up behind, reading slogans like "Coffin Joe: A Candidate with a Pulse" and "A Chicken in Every Pot, a Body in Every Grave!"

JOSEPH COFFIN, *dressed as a Grim Reaper in a suit, steps up to the podium. Reporters in front row flash bulbs, hold up microphones.*

COFFIN: Hello, thank you for coming on such short notice. I have a brief statement and then I'll take questions. My fellow citizens, over the past few weeks there have been many allegations about my conduct in the office of Grim Reaper. I want to reassure everyone - these charges are not true! I did not accept bribes. I did not rig afterlife sentencing, and I am still running for President! Now, if anyone would like to ask a few quest— *(The flashing gets faster, and the journalists raise their microphones higher.)*

JOURNALISTS: Mr. Reaper! Mr. Reaper!

COFFIN: One at a time, please! One at a time! You there, Frank!

FRANK: Thank you, sir; Frank Stein, for *66 Minutes.* You mentioned the allegations of bribery, that you accepted payment of souls from prominent members of society in return for lighter sentencing in the afterlife…

COFFIN: Yes, I'm aware of the charges. I know how serious human soul trafficking is in this day and age, and I would never—

FRANK: But the charges don't accuse you of trafficking in *human* souls, Mr. Reaper. They state that you accepted bribes paid in *vampire* souls. Any comment? *(Everyone leans their mikes in.)*

COFFIN: *(Clearing his throat.)* Uh… I… As far as I know, Frank, vampires are classified as undead, and… uh… therefore they wouldn't actually have souls to accept as bribery. *(Everyone murmurs and types as flashes increase.)*

FRANK: I'm sorry, sir, did you just say vampires don't have souls?

COFFIN: Uh… No, uh… That's not what I meant, uh… That is to say, uh… No comment! *(COFFIN runs off, and all the journalists turn around while cameras and microphones are put in front of them.)*

JOURNALIST 1: You heard it here, listeners! This is *MPR News*, and we've got the latest in the scandal erupting over incumbent Grim Reaper Joseph Coffin!

JOURNALIST 2: Tonight at eleven! First, it was bribery! Afterlife corruption! And now— Soulgate! Does Joseph Coffin really believe that vampires don't have souls?

FRANK: An embattled public official, called by some the next possible President, caught on tape taking bribes and accusing Transylvanian Americans of being less… than living beings. This story and the ghost of Andy Rooney tonight on *66 Minutes*! *(Man in glasses and suit, ARI WESTPHAL, comes out and shoos everyone off stage.)*

ARI: Alright, alright! That's enough, everyone! You've got your headlines! Everybody out of here!

JOURNALIST 3: Hey, Ari! *Gallows Gazette*! Care to give our readers a comment?

ARI: Yeah. Go buy a better paper! The *Gazette*'s nothing but a hack tabloid!

JOURNALIST 3: My foot, it is! Best in the tri-state! We just beat out the *Infernal Inquirer* in sales!

ARI: Get lost! Print journalism is dead anyway!

JOURNALIST 3: Who cares if it's dead? We sell more papers than anyone in the graveyard! (*Everyone but ARI exits. COFFIN comes back on.*)

COFFIN: Are they all gone?

ARI: Yes. Yes, they're gone, Mr. Reaper.

COFFIN: Please, Ari. Call me Joe. You're my chief of staff, not my teacher.

ARI: No, I'm your "campaign crisis manager." Don't call me your chief of staff in public. That would make me a government worker, and that would make me open to subpoena!

COFFIN: Okay, okay. Well, if you're my crisis manager, then start managing! I can't take any more questions like this! They're making me look like a monster!

ARI: Sir, you're the Grim Reaper. Of course, you look like a monster.

COFFIN: Hey, I was elected Grim Reaper, wasn't I? The people wanted me to manage life or death decisions, go after the bad souls and look after the good ones. But now they start calling me corrupt?

ARI: Joe, you've gotta relax. It's a 24-hour news story. Just wait a day or two, and the reporters will find something else to investigate.

COFFIN: If it's a 24-hour news story, how come it takes a day or two?

ARI: Eh, 24 hours in business days. I don't make the rules. Time zones in the afterlife are very confusing.

COFFIN: Well, you've got to get them off my back now. I need a fighter. Get me Mitsy Morte!

ARI: Joe, Mitsy Morte isn't just a fighter. She's a fixer. She's one of the shadiest lawyers in the business. If you hire her, everybody will think you're guilty!

COFFIN: I don't care what they think as long as I win! And Mitsy Morte wins cases! You see how she handled that Zombie Class Action?

ARI: Oh, c'mon! She got those zombies off on a technicality! The court didn't rule they were innocent of eating brains, only that they had a right to eat brains because of a medical condition!

COFFIN: Look, I've made up my mind. I need these stories gone.

ARI: You don't need to worry about it! I promise, in a week, nobody's gonna even remember this business with the souls, and the bribery, and the vampires. And if I'm not right, may God strike me— *(Before he finishes talking a **COURIER** walks up to them.)*

COURIER: Excuse me, are you Joe Coffin? District Grim Reaper?

COFFIN: Yes, I am. What, another question from the press?

COURIER: Oh, no! I'm not with the press! I hate those guys!

ARI: Then who are you?

COURIER: Court courier. Subpoena. *(Hands them a blue envelope.)* You've been served. *(**COURIER** walks off. **COFFIN** looks at **ARI** smirking.)*

ARI: I'll call her! Okay? I'll call her!

COFFIN: Good. Good! Now. What's up next on the schedule?

ARI: You've got a meeting with the Furies Union at 11 and then a luncheon with the Daughters of the Pandemonium Revolution at 1.

COFFIN: Okay. Oh, and make sure you get the driver to stop on the way for a hamburger or something, okay? Demon food is a little too rich for my stomach…

ARI: Duly noted. *(**COFFIN** & **ARI** exit.)*

SCENE 2: Mitsy Morte's Law Office

MITSY MORTE's law office has brown brick walls and a law degree hanging in a frame, law books sitting in half assembled IKEA-style furniture, and a desk that is propped up by one or two books on one leg. Large windows overlook a city scene, with MITSY MORTE's desk in front, a chair with its back turned to the audience.

MITSY: *(She sits with her back turned to the stage in a big rolling chair, talking on the phone.)* Yes, Johnny… Johnny! You know I love you, but your case is so full of holes you could sell it in a farmer's market as Swiss cheese! You gotta take the deal. And don't blame me. You're the one who got caught on a wiretap. An angel wiretap! They're always listening! Worse than Santa Claus. *(MITSY's assistant LUPINA enters, and motions to MITSY.)*

LUPINA: Miss Morte? You busy?

MITSY: It's just Johnny Faust. Again. Idiot sold his soul to the Devil in return for a date with Marilyn Monroe. Then she shows up, and she's not a blonde, so he wants to void the contract.

LUPINA: But Marilyn Monroe wasn't a blonde. She dyed it.

MITSY: I know. You try telling that to the Faust kid. *(To phone.)* Look— you're gonna have to do time, but it'll only be Limbo! Minimum security! It's a country club without air conditioning. *(She hangs up.)* Okay! So, what's up?

LUPINA: Ari Westphal, he's crisis manager to the District Grim Reaper.

MITSY: Ooh! Ari! He's still around? Right. Let him in. *(LUPINA exits, and ARI comes in, sighing. MITSY stands up with her arms out.)*

MITSY: Ari! Darling! How've you been?

ARI: Don't even try it, Mitsy! I'm not in the mood!

MITSY: I bet you're in a mood! You wouldn't have come to me if you weren't desperate!

ARI: Go ahead. Rub it in. Get it over with. It'll save us time. I have a case for you…

MITSY: Yeah, I heard. Good ol' Coffin Joe! I love those campaign signs you did. "At midnight, I'll possess your vote!" Classic!

ARI: Sure, classic. Truth be told, we only won because Mothman split the vote for us against the Mole Men.

MITSY: Well, what's he got to worry about? Tell me everything. Pretend I don't watch the news. Treat me like I'm only 300 years old.

ARI: Okay. The District Grim Reaper handles all the afterlife-related cases. They decide whether or not it's somebody's time to die, and then they sentence where they go after that.

MITSY: Where did they go? Like which cemetery? You're telling me you need a license to go to the graveyard?

ARI: No, Grim Reaper sends you to your afterlife, depending on your record. Sometimes that means heaven, sometimes reincarnation. It all depends on which religion someone belongs to.

MITSY: Oh yeah! I had a case against you guys when I was representing a scientist! He sure was mad where you guys sent him!

ARI: The one who invented a cure for zombies? We sent him to heaven!

MITSY: Yeah, but he was an atheist. Good thing he paid well; he was annoying.

ARI: Well, that's the least of your worries. Half the time, we aren't sending people to heaven.

MITSY: You're talking about The Other Place? It's not so bad. We went there for my second honeymoon. They even had a Disneyland! But it was nothing but lines going on for eternity.

ARI: So here's the problem. Whenever Joe's running for office, he has to get campaign contributions. And everybody who donates to our campaign always wants a few… favors.

MITSY: Let me guess—people donate to you and want you to keep them off the list going to The Other Place.

ARI: Not exactly. This is all… hypothetical, okay? But let's just say we get more money from… The Other Place.

MITSY: *(Fake shock.)* No! And what, they want you to send them more souls?

ARI: No, not more souls! Less! They ran out of room down there back when Nixon took us off the gold standard.

MITSY: So what do you do with the souls who were supposed to go there?

ARI: Well… And this is just hypothetical, mind you… We have to get a little creative there. Find different mythologies where they might fit in. We send homicidal maniacs to Valhalla—the Vikings are pretty chill about that sort of thing as long as we say they're warriors.

MITSY: What about lawyers? Where do you send them?

ARI: Oh, they go straight to The Other Place. No exceptions.

MITSY: Fair enough… but it sounds like all these other afterlife places must be angry.

ARI: That's what we just got hit with! A class action lawsuit from eighty-six of the major world religions ordering us to cease and desist from sending souls to them!

MITSY: Okay. You've definitely got yourself a case here. But what am I supposed to do about it? I mean, I'm just a good old-fashioned country lawyer…

ARI: Look, Mitsy, I don't like you. But you're a shark. The worst of the worst. You know every dirty trick in the book. And maybe that's just what we need right now.

MITSY: Ari, Ari, you had me at "worst of the worst." Lupina! Get in here! *(LUPINA re-enters.)* Ari, I'm gonna start by putting my girl Lupina on this. Lupina, I want you to investigate the vampire angle with the Grim Reaper case.

LUPINA: Right, boss.

ARI: Wait, the vampires? I mean, sure the press has been talking about that, but they're just a small part of the case…

LUPINA: No, vampires are always the best place to start investigating.

ARI: Why?

LUPINA: Because they like to talk. The longer you live, the more likely you are to brag.

MITSY: Yeah, like they say. Vampires never keep their mouths shut!

ARI: Sounds a lot like you, Mitsy.

MITSY: Eh, I'm only vampire on my mother's side. But I'm still a blood sucker– a blood sucking lawyer!

ARI: Don't remind me... *(MITSY, LUPINA, and ARI exit.)*

SCENE 3: Law Firm

*An expensive, swanky-looking law firm, in direct contrast to the ramshackle look of **MITSY**'s office. Tasteful beige walls and carpets, modern art paintings on the walls, and a chic-looking logo for DC&H.*

*Two head lawyers, **DIANA DEWEY** and **HOWARD HOW**E, sit at a table with several junior associates and their clients, **KEVIN MEPHISTO** and **DAVID MARCATO**, who wear devil horns.*

DEWEY: Alright, let's go over everything before the plaintiff's people get here. Howard, do you know where Chester is?

HOWE: He says he's in traffic. There was an accident up on I-66.

DEWEY: Oh my. Is he hurt?

HOWE: No, he just wanted to stop by the car crash to see if anybody wanted a lawyer.

DEWEY: Good for him. He gives ambulance chasers a good name.

HOWE: Well, from the sound of it, I think this is more like chasing hearses.

DEWEY: Either way, a client's a client.

MEPHISTO: Um, excuse me. But aren't we your clients, too?

MARCATO: The ADLU is paying for three name partners to be on this case, not just two!

HOWE: Why? Because you want all your invoices to be multiples of three?

DEWEY: Gentlemen, you don't have to worry. My partner will be here soon, and everybody on this case will give one-hundred percent to the American Devil Liberties Union's case.

HOWE: And don't worry! We'll make sure our billable hourly rate will be $666!

ASSOCIATE 1: Ma'am? There's someone here for you.

DEWEY: Ah, good. Chester's here?

ASSOCIATE 1: Uh, that's not what I— *(MITSY enters, pushing the ASSOCIATE out of the way.)*

MITSY: Hello, Diana! Did you miss me?

DEWEY: Mitsy Morte! Of all the backstabbing, doublecrossing—

MITSY: Please, please. Flattery will get you everywhere. How've you been?

MEPHISTO: You know this woman?

HOWE: Yeah, that's Mitsy Morte. One of the most conniving, cold-blooded, low-down dirty demons who ever passed the bar!

MARCATO: Sounds like we should've hired her.

DEWEY: Don't give her any ideas! Mitsy, I don't know what you're doing here, but you're not going to steal another one of our clients! Who even let you in here? *(CHESTER enters, smiling broadly.)*

CHESTER: I did!

MITSY: There you are! Where'd you go?

CHESTER: Oh, I just needed to pick up a bagel. You want a bagel?

MITSY: Oh no, I'm on the Seven Deadly Sins Diet.

CHESTER: *(To DIANA.)* I ran into Mitsy on the way up in the elevator. You know our case against the Grim Reaper? She's on the other side!

HOWE: Great. Just great.

CHESTER: Oh c'mon, Howard! This is gonna be fun!

DEWEY: Well, now that we're all caught up, let's get started. *(Everyone sits down. An ASSOCIATE sets up a camera.)*

DEWEY: Are we recording? Good. Ahem. Let the record show that I am Diana Dewey, head attorney.

CHESTER: Chester Cheatam.

HOWE: Howard Howe.

DEWEY: Of the firm of Dewey...

CHESTER: Cheatam...

HOWE: And Howe!

DEWEY: And we represent the American Devil Liberties Union in this matter against the District Grim Reaper, Joseph L. Coffin III, on the matter of illegalities surrounding the distribution of souls.

MITSY: Are you done? (*DEWEY nods.*) Good. Okay, uh... I'm Mitsy Morte... I like long walks on the beach and Italian cinema...

HOWE. (*Exasperated*): Will you stop it?

MITSY: And I'm here to represent good ol' Coffin Joe on the matter of... everything you just said.

DEWEY: Would it KILL you to take this seriously?

MITSY: (*Gesturing to MARCATO and MEPHISTO.*) If it did, I guess I'd have to go to YOU guys to represent me, wouldn't I, boys? Or does the ADLU handle cases for lesser demons like me?

MEPHISTO: Uh...

MITSY: Okay, technically I'm HALF demon on my dad's side... half Angel of Death on my mom's side... I think there's some chupacabra mixed in somewhere. I'm a real mutt. Not a purebred pedigree demon like YOUR clients...

MEPHISTO: Now, see here...

MARCATO: Technically we represent ALL demons in the lowerarchy whenever they face significant challenges to their afterlife related legal statuses, though we prioritize—

MITSY: Let me guess– you prioritize the demons who get mentioned in rock songs and movies and want a bigger cut of the money, am I right?

MEPHISTO: Hey! That's no laughing matter!

MARCATO: Do you have any idea how much residuals that band was refusing to pay Beelzebub until we got them to pay out?

MITSY: Sure, sure, but you boys ain't exactly looking for charity cases, is what I mean!

HOWE: Mitsy, please. You're not one to talk about this.

CHESTER: Yeah, you used to handle all the "Crossroad Contracts" we had with entertainers looking to sell their souls for fortune and glory.

HOWE: Before you up and stabbed us in the back, that is!

MITSY: Hey, I made sure I put a good ol' fashioned Escape Clause loophole in those contracts so none of those musicians ever had to do a day down in the hot place for selling their souls!

HOWE: Sure, you just made sure they spent a couple centuries in Purgatory instead. And for a handy profit, I might add.

MITSY: Okay, one– Purgatory's better than The Other Place. And two– technically speaking while I was working here, you guys got the Purgatorial tax-write off. Heck, probably paid for the new office remodeling!

DEWEY: *(To CHESTER and HOWE.)* She's got a point...

MITSY: Look, we could spend all day biting at each other's throats, but I'm a busy gal, so let's skip to the good stuff. How much do you want for a settlement? *(DEWEY, HOWE, & CHESTER look surprised.)*

DEWEY: A... A settlement? Already?

MITSY: Let's be real. You're gonna highball me. I'm gonna lowball you. It'll be easier for us to get to the end of this if you just tell me what the ceiling is on this lawsuit.

DEWEY: That's not how this works, Mitsy. First, we're going to—

MEPHISTO: We want thirty three million in compensatory damages, with another in punitive!

CHESTER: Gentlemen! Please! We're the lawyers. We do the talking.

MARCATO: I'm sorry! She's just so convincing!

MITSY: Wow. Sixty-six mill. That's quite a lot of money.

HOWE: And divisible by three. See, what'd I tell you?

DEWEY: Let's get one thing straight, Mitsy. That's not the ceiling for us. It's the floor. No, strike that; it's the basement. Your client accepted bribes to send thousands of souls away from their final destinations into new and unfamiliar afterlives that have left them profoundly traumatized!

MITSY: Traumatized? My client sent them to the nice afterlives! What, they would've rather gone to The Other Place?

MEPHISTO: Don't act so surprised. The District Grim Reaper sent our clients into afterlives they had no idea how to fit in with! They didn't know the customs, didn't speak the language!

MARCATO: One of our clients got eaten by an alligator because he didn't read the Egyptian Book of the Dead! How was he supposed to keep his heart from getting heavier than a feather?

MITSY: See, this is why I started a diet.

DEWEY: As you can see, our clients are not happy. And we're not happy. And we won't be happy until your client agrees to pay 66 million.

MITSY: Okay. See, here's the thing. My client's already told me a figure he's happy with, and it's the most I'm allowed to negotiate for.

HOWE: Okay, let's see it.

DEWEY: Howard! We're not moving from 66 million!

HOWE: Pfffff. As long as I get my cut, I don't care.

MITSY: *(Pulling out a check.)* Okay, here it is. *(She hands it to DIANA. She and CHESTER stare at it.)*

DEWEY: It says… "Pay to the order of… Zero zero comma zero zero zero comma zero zero zero dollars…"

CHESTER: "And zero cents."

HOWE: Well. At least it's the right number of zeroes.

MITSY: Actually, two more! So I'm being generous, really.

DEWEY: We'll see you in court.

MITSY: Actually, no. I don't think you will.

CHESTER: What's that supposed to mean?

MITSY: It means that subpoena you sent me? I looked it over. Gave it a good read through. And then I put it in the shredder.

HOWE: Great! You just got slapped with a fine, which adds more to our fees!

MITSY: Not exactly. Because see, here's the thing. When you filed a class action lawsuit against my client, the District Grim Reaper, you had to undersign it with all the names of the plaintiffs in your case, and you only mentioned the American Devil Liberties Union…

MEPHISTO: That's right! We're one of the oldest and most trusted legal institutions in the country!

MARCATO: Well, one of the oldest, anyway.

MITSY: Yeah, but that's just one plaintiff. You need more than one for it to be a class action.

DEWEY: Yes, but obviously, they represent the whole of the plaintiffs in the matter against—

MITSY: Actually, they don't! Because I took the liberty of calling up some of those plaintiffs before I came here, and… they said they'd never heard of any class action.

CHESTER: What's she talking about?

MEPHISTO: Well… Uh… We're doing this on their behalf! There's no need to involve them in any of the paperwork!

MITSY: What about the sixty-six million payout? I guess there wouldn't be any need to involve them in that paperwork, either, huh?

MARCATO: Now, see here! We filed that lawsuit perfectly according to the laws of the Ninth Circuit Court of Appeals!

MITSY: No, you see here! This action against my client is bogus, and unless you want to get brought up on disciplinary charges, I suggest you reconsider your case! Now, if you'll excuse me, I think I'll go get myself a bagel. (*Exits.*)

HOWE: What's that mean? Somebody tell me what this means!

DEWEY: It means she played us, Howard.

CHESTER: Oh, this is good. This is really good.

HOWE: How can you be happy, you idiot? She just schooled us in front of our clients!

CHESTER: You wanna know why I'm happy? Because she still thinks she can win! And she has no idea what kind of aces we have up our sleeves… *(To **MEPHISTO** and **MARCATO**.)* Fellas, I think it's time we call your buddies in HSA.

MEPHISTO: The HSA? Really?

MARCATO: Do you really think it's wise for us to bring them in? I mean, we could get in a lot of trouble if we contact them…

CHESTER: Oh, come on. You'll be fine. You said you guys have friends in high places…

SCENE 4: Teppes Gardens

*Teppes Gardens is an apartment building in an expensive district. A plaque on the wall outside the entrance reads, "Founded in 1897." **LUPINA** and **ARI** sit outside in a parked car under a street sign that plainly says, "Don't even think about parking here." An intimidating-looking gargoyle doorman blocks the entrance. **DOORMAN** stands at the entrance door.*

ARI: Okay, so how do we do this, exactly?

LUPINA: How do we do what, exactly?

ARI: Uh…This! Sitting here and waiting for this guy to show up! That's what you do on a stake out, right?

LUPINA: You might want to be careful about using the words "stake out" when we're in front of the wealthiest vampire on the east coast…

ARI: Oh, you know what I mean! *(Frowns.)* Are you really sure this is the guy we should be talking to?

LUPINA: You said Coffin Joe was worried about how the vampire community would react to his interview, didn't you?

ARI: I said it was nothing! Nothing at all!

LUPINA: Except you're worried they might pull their money from the campaign.

ARI: Hey, I didn't say that! I never said anything like that! And I never would either! And more importantly… *(Looks both ways.)* Where did you hear that?

LUPINA: Easy, Ari. You don't want to raise your blood pressure. It's pretty simple. Coffin Joe was an outsider before he was elected. Neither party wanted him.

ARI: That's right! He's not some political puppet. He's a man of the people!

LUPINA: Which is why the majority of his political donations were from bonds that were written out back during the 1800s.

ARI: Wait, what?

LUPINA: It's all in public record. Coffin Joe's biggest donors during the election all had bank accounts that dated back to the Civil War. Only people who could have accounts like that are vampires.

ARI: Only vampires? Wait, what about werewolves?

LUPINA: *(Confused.)* I dunno, Ari. What about werewolves?

ARI: I mean, weren't there werewolves in the Civil War, too?

LUPINA: Sure, but they wouldn't still be alive today. Werewolves aren't immortal, Ari.

ARI: They're not?

LUPINA: No! At least not the ones on my dating app.

ARI: Okay, okay. But what about witches? They're immortal, right?

LUPINA: Some of them– yes. But even if they were, they were staying underground back then. Still too close to the whole "burning at the stake" era of history.

ARI: Okay, okay. Oh, how about demons? It could be a demon with the account, right?

LUPINA: Good point, good point. There's plenty of demons who would've been around back then. But, here's the thing. These are Confederate bank accounts. And even demons didn't fight for those guys.

ARI: Ah, ah yeah… What about Angels?

LUPINA: Let's not even go there. *(Waving her hand.)* Occam's Razor says the simplest answer tends to be the right one. And in this case, the simplest answer is…

ARI: …Vampires.

LUPINA: Right. But don't worry, I'm prepared.

ARI: Prepared? What's that mean?

LUPINA: In the glove compartment I've got two quarts of holy water, can of garlic spray, and a crucifix. If those don't work, in the trunk I've got wooden stakes, silver swords, and a baseball bat.

ARI: A baseball bat? Look, I understand the holy water, the garlic, and everything else. But since when are vampires afraid of baseball bats?

LUPINA: Everybody's afraid of baseball bats.

ARI: Okay, don't tell me anything else, I don't wanna know. In case we get arrested, I mean! I just hope you're not wearing a wire...

LUPINA: Relax, I'd never wear a wire. First they have to tape it on you, then the glue gets everywhere, and when you rip it off, say goodbye to your fur...

ARI: Fur? What fur?

LUPINA: Well, during a full moon, anyway.

ARI: Wait...Oh, you're a werewolf! But what do you do during a full moon?

LUPINA: Hmm... Speed dating, mostly.

ARI: Cool...Wait, something's up... (*A gaudy billionaire, **DONNY NOSFERATU**, comes out, wearing an expensive suit and sunglasses and carrying an umbrella.*)

DOORMAN: Good afternoon, sir.

DONNY: Jimmy! How you doin' kid?

DOORMAN: Uh, I'm not Jimmy, sir. I'm Billy.

DONNY: Yeah, whatever. (*Offering him a wad of bills.*) I need my car pulled up. Can you do that for me, Jimmy?

DOORMAN: (*Taking the money.*) Whatever you say, sir. (*The **DOORMAN** leaves, and **ARI** and **LUPINA** get out.*)

LUPINA: Now's our chance. (*To **DONNY**.*) Excuse me, sir? Are you Mister Nosferatu?

DONNY: Mister Nosferatu? Nonononono. Call me Donny. MISTER Nosferatu was my father's name! Well, actually it was Count, but nobody talks like that here in the States, knowwhatImean?

ARI: Great. Real charming.

LUPINA *(To ARI.)*: He's your fundraiser. *(To DONNY.)* Right, Donny. My friend and I are with Joseph Coffin's campaign. Can we talk to you for a minute?

DONNY: Who? Ah, right! Good ol' Coffin Joe! Sure, ask me anything you want, but make it quick. I got tickets to a ball game.

ARI: *(Under his breath.)* Let me guess; it's a night game.

LUPINA: Well, we don't want to keep you, so tell us this. You're still organizing Mister Coffin's Political Action Committee, aren't you?

DONNY: Sure, sure. Coffin JoePAC. But...I thought I wasn't allowed to coordinate with you guys. Officially, I mean.

ARI: That's right. You aren't. But we are allowed to ask you questions... hypothetically...

DONNY: Oh, I get ya! Right! Nice little loop-hole there!

ARI: Right, well. Hypothetically... If Coffin Joe happened to say anything about his constituents... How do you think they would respond?

DONNY: Well, what type of constituents are we talking about here, hypothetically?

ARI: His vampire constituents. His billionaire vampire campaign contributor constituents.

DONNY: Right, right. Look—My old man, he had to worry about villagers comin' after him with the pitchforks, and the torches, you know what I mean? So we get called a few names on TV! Hypothetically. So what!

ARI: Okay, good! So that means our funders are happy! We don't have to worry about them leaving!

LUPINA: Hold on a sec...*(To DONNY.)* Do you mean that...hypothetically?

DONNY: Huh? What's she talking about?

LUPINA: This is all just hypothetical, remember? You can't coordinate with us officially, but as long as it's all hypothetical you can tell us the truth about anything. So, the members of JoePAC are happy...Hypothetically?

DONNY: Look, say it any which way you want, I don't have time to keep talking with you if I wanna make that game, okay? Ari, you call me sometime!

ARI: Hold on, Donny! *(To LUPINA.)* Lupina, what are you doing?

LUPINA: Just hang on a sec. I've got an idea. *(She goes over to the car. The DOORMAN comes back on.)*

DONNY: Jeez, Ari. Where'd you find this girl? Under a rock?

ARI: Almost. At a law firm.

DOORMAN: Excuse me, Donny. Your car is waiting at the corner.

DONNY: Thanks, Jimmy! Now look, Ari, I gotta run. I don't have time to-- WOAH! *(LUPINA comes back carrying a baseball bat. The DOORMAN stands in her way.)*

ARI: Lupina! Are you crazy? Put that thing down!

LUPINA: Just a second, Ari! *(To DOORMAN.)* Excuse me sir, may I pass?

DOORMAN: I'm afraid not, miss. I'll have you know that I'm not only this building's doorman, but I'm also a bodyguard. I have black belts in kung fu, jiu jitsu, and three forbidden schools of ninja karate! I won't let any harm come to Mister Nosferatu!

LUPINA: Don't worry. I'm not interested in Mister Nosferatu. I'm interested in his car.

DOORMAN: Oh. Go right ahead then, miss.

DONNY: My car? What does she want with my... *(LUPINA goes offstage. Sound effects of glass breaking and car smashing, and a car alarm being set off. DONNY screams, and is held back by ARI.)* NO! My car! My beautiful car! Somebody stop her, please! Jimmy, stop her!

DOORMAN: Sorry, sir. I'm your doorman. Not your chauffeur.

DONNY: Ari, please, you can't let her do this! It's a Rolls-Royce!

ARI: Look, Donny, I'm afraid I can't really do anything about it.

DONNY: But it's not just a car! It's my baby! I'm one of your biggest contributors!

ARI: I know, I know, Donny. But you know the rules! Legally speaking I can't coordinate with our PAC. Not officially anyway.

DONNY: Okay, okay! I'll talk, I'll tell you what you wanna know, okay? Just make her stop!

ARI: Sure thing. Lupina! *(ARI motions, and the crashing stops. LUPINA strolls onstage, holding a keychain. She clicks it, and the car alarm stops. She tosses the keys back to DONNY, who fumbles as he catches them.)*

LUPINA: There. Don't worry, it's just a few dents. And some body damage. Windows, mirrors, hazard lights. I think the hood ornament's still okay…

DONNY: Enough already! You've done your dirty work! *(Sniffling.)* You wanna know why all the campaign donors are leaving Coffin Joe, don't you?

ARI: Leaving! So they are leaving? But you said—

DONNY: I said what I had to! And I almost got away with it, too!

ARI: Jeez! I knew it! So Joe really did get you guys mad with the souls comment!

DONNY: What, the souls thing? Nah, nah! Nobody cared about that! Us vampires have been looking for an excuse to ditch Coffin Joe a while now. This whole soul thing just seemed like a good excuse.

ARI: But why? Coffin Joe's always done right by the vampire community! He's been making sure you guys have a good afterlife plan set up! He's gotten nine out of ten major religions to stop calling vampires unholy demons of the night!

DONNY: Look, we don't care about any of that stuff! We care about the money!

ARI: The money?

DONNY: Sure, the money! I mean, c'mon! All of us vampires made our fortunes back in the middle ages. Why do you think vampires are all living in mansions and spooky castles, and whatnot?

ARI: Alright, so what about the money? You've got enough to donate, don't you?

DONNY: Sure, and that would be fine, if it weren't for Coffin Joe and his Death Tax!

ARI: Death Tax?

DONNY: That's right! He's the Grim Reaper, so he hits vampire incomes with a Death Tax because, technically speaking, we're all dead!

ARI: But that's only a five percent tax, isn't it? You can afford to pay that, can't you?

DONNY: Afford to pay it? I'd rather pay twice as much not to pay it!

LUPINA: That… doesn't make sense.

DONNY: Of course it doesn't make sense! It's politics! And it's why we're leaving Coffin Joe! We want to find someone who'll only tax us to death, not tax us after death!

LUPINA: So if the vampires are pulling out of Coffin Joe's campaign, who are they joining?

DONNY: Look, you didn't hear it from me, but word is, a new candidate is about to join the race! A dark horse candidate. And they're gonna blow Coffin Joe out of the water. Now, if you'll excuse me! *(To LUPINA.)* Mark my words, girl! I will have my revenge.

LUPINA: Alright, choose your weapon. Sword? Flintlock?

DONNY: Worse! Attorney! *(Storms off.)*

LUPINA: Good thing for me I keep Mitsy on retainer.

ARI: This is great! This is just great! A dark horse candidate. Just what we need!

LUPINA: Yeah. And that's not all.

ARI: Oh? What else?

LUPINA: I'm gonna have to get a new bat.

SCENE 5: 66 Minutes Television Studio

A television studio, filled with wires, lights hanging everywhere, boom microphones and cameras with a CBS-styled eye logo, but with a sinister vertical cat eye slit. A sign in the background bears a clock with the logo for 66 Minutes. **COFFIN JOE** *sits across from a camera while news people fit him for a microphone and do make-up.* **MITSY** *paces across the room meanwhile.* **PRODUCTION ASSISTANTS** *can be seen fiddling with camera/studio equipment in the background, maybe reviewing clipboards and talking with each other.*

MITSY: *(On phone.)* Maddie…? Maddie, are you there…? Yes, Maddie I can hear you. Just meet us at the studio and we'll talk then. Bye.

NEWSGIRL 1: Okay, just hold still, Mister District Reaper. We need to make sure everything's ready for the interview.

NEWSGIRL 2: Ready, steady.

COFFIN: Right, what are you setting up right now, the mike?

NEWSGIRL 1: Oh, we already have that sir. Now we have to do your make-up.

NEWSGIRL 2: Little blush here, a little powder there…

COFFIN: You don't need to make me look good on camera! I'm a regular joe!

NEWSGIRL 1: You're also the Grim Reaper, sir. To be quite frank, we don't even know if you'll show up on the camera.

NEWSGIRL 2: Gotta make you look lifelike.

COFFIN: Look, kid, why don't you give us the room? I need to talk to my attorney before the interview, okay?

NEWSGIRL 1: Don't wanna listen to us? Fine. It's your funeral!

NEWSGIRL 2: Pick a casket, why don't you. *(Both **NEWSGIRLS** leave.)*

MITSY: Okay, look Joe. This case is gonna be bigger than I thought, so I called in the big guns.

COFFIN: Big guns? But I thought you were the big guns!

MITSY: Sure, if you're going up against a militia, I am! But if Dewey, Cheatam, and Howe were telling the truth, you're going up against a ballistic missile!

COFFIN: So there's gonna be a class action. Big deal! The ADLU isn't in it for the money. They're looking for publicity! Soon as this hits the newsstands, they'll settle nice and easy.

MITSY: Maybe. And maybe it'll leave you open for something bigger.

COFFIN: There's nothing else you need to worry about. Don't you trust me?

MITSY: Trust you? Joe, I'm your lawyer! Of course I don't trust you! *(Phone rings.)* Hold on. Hello? Hello, Maddie? Are you here yet? We're on the third floor!

MADDIE: *(Offstage.)* Hello? Hello, Mitsy? Where are you?

MITSY: Oh, for the love of. *(Yelling.)* Over here, Maddie!

COFFIN: Exactly what kind of lawyer is this girl supposed to be if she can't figure out how a phone works?

MITSY: Her name's Maddie Sinclair, and she's the best there is, trust me! Just… Don't look her in the eye too much. It makes her uncomfortable.

COFFIN: Why, what is she? Some kind of— *(MADDIE SINCLAIR enters, wearing sunglasses and her hair a nest full of snakes. COFFIN JOE averts his eyes.)* Oh, no! Not one of them!

MITSY: Shush, you! *(To MADDIE.)* Maddie! How are you? I haven't seen you since my last disbarment!

MADDIE: There's always the next one! And is that Coffin Joe? Oh, hello sir! I voted for you in the last election!

COFFIN. *(Outraged)*: Mitsy, are you out of your mind? You brought a Medusa in here?

MITSY: Joe! Shame on you! They're not all called Medusa!

MADDIE: Actually Maddie is short for Medusa. But it's an old family name. I'm a Gorgon! Haven't you seen Clash of the Titans? My mom was a model for Ray Harryhausen!

COFFIN: Yeah, seen it! Specifically the part where they turn people into stone when they look at you!

MITSY: Oh, come on! That's just an old wives' tale! ...Isn't it?

MADDIE: I think so! I mean, I've never turned anybody into stone just by looking at them! Sure, I've gotten plenty of stares, and awkward pauses, and occasionally people ask if they can touch my hair for some reason.

MITSY: Really? What do you say then?

MADDIE: I tell them it's a bad idea if they didn't bring any anti-venom injections with them. *(NEWSGIRLS comes on with FRANK.)*

NEWSGIRL 1: Mr. Coffin? We're ready to tape!

NEWSGIRL 2: Don't look at the camera.

MADDIE: Don't worry about me, sir. I'm just here to observe. I'll stand back, watch, you won't even know I'm here!

COFFIN: I wish I didn't...

(MADDIE and MITSY stand back as JOE joins FRANK.)

MITSY: So, how's he look?

MADDIE: Hold on. Let's see how he talks before I say how bad it is.

MITSY: "How bad?" It's not even a question of good or bad?

MADDIE: Honey, I'm the second lawyer you called in here. If this case gets any worse you won't need any more lawyers, you'll need a priest.

PRODUCTION ASSISTANT 1 and 2: Quiet on the set!

PRODUCTION ASSISTANT 1: Get ready to rock and roll, people!

PRODUCTION ASSISTANT 2: And we're on in five, four, three, two…

FRANK: Tonight, on 66 *Minutes*, we examine the case of District Reaper, Mister Joseph Coffin, known to voters as "Coffin Joe." He's running for President, and everyone wants to know…why? Thank you for speaking with us, Mister Reaper.

COFFIN: Call me Joe.

MADDIE: Ooh, bad sign.

MITSY: Why's that a bad sign?

MADDIE: Politicians are only that friendly if they have something to hide.

FRANK: Let's talk about your life before running for office. Isn't it true that you were one of the top lawyers in the underworld, at the firm of Screwtape & Associates?

COFFIN: Well, I don't know if I was one of the top lawyers, but I was certainly one of the most efficient. Eighty-eight cases in five years, and I always got my clients the best possible outcome.

FRANK: But you weren't undefeated. In fact, it says here that you actually pled out all your cases.

COFFIN: You have to understand, we're talking about people who'd been charged with major offenses, all the major seven deadly sins. Gluttony, Greed, Wrath, Sloth—you've seen the movie, right?

FRANK: Sure, sure.

COFFIN: And it was my job to make sure my clients didn't get the Good Book thrown at them just because they'd, y'know, made a few mistakes.

MITSY: See? Sounds like he knows how to spin a story.

MADDIE: Just as long as it doesn't spin out of control...

FRANK: So, what kinds of sins were your clients pleading down from?

COFFIN: Look, I can't really go into specifics without violating confidentiality...

FRANK: Fraud? Treason? Crimes against humanity?

COFFIN: Well...*(Waves his hands.)* I mean it's not like most of them were even "human" to begin with...

MADDIE: Aaaaaaaaand here we go.

FRANK: Let's talk about the job you have now. As State District Reaper, you're on the opposite side of the same cases you were working on as a defense attorney. Instead of defending accused souls, you're trying to put them away and send them to The Other Place.

COFFIN: That's right. And my office has a spotless record of—

FRANK: That's why these records obtained by *66 Minutes* are so troubling. Would you care to look at them?

COFFIN: Uh...I don't have my reading glasses...

FRANK: *(Pointing at papers.)* I'll direct you to this passage here. These bank records indicate you received massive payments from your clients to get them sent to heaven. All this while you sent low income souls to The Other Place for sins like...jaywalking...cursing and...giving good reviews to bad movies?

COFFIN: Hey, we're getting a lot of movie bloggers! You can't let people who think the 90s *Dracula* is better than the original go to heaven!

FRANK: Isn't this just more of the same, Joe? Only the wealthy get to go to heaven. The rich get richer, and the poor get...well done?

COFFIN: First of all, you show my office respect and call me Mister District Reaper. Secondly—

MADDIE: Okay! That's it! Interview's over!

FRANK: But we just got started!

MADDIE: Oh, you've got everything you want already! You'll probably cut half of that out anyway and cut to commercial!

NEWSGIRL 1: But what about B-Roll?

MITSY: You heard the lady! Out of here, right now! All of you! We need to talk to our client.

FRANK: You're making a big mistake! You don't want to get journalists against you! We're here to inform the public against tyrants and dictators. We'll expose all your secrets the more you try and cover them up!

MADDIE: Beat it! Or I'll have my snakes give you the evil eye! *(FRANK, NEWSGIRLS, & PRODUCTION ASSISTANTS exit.)*

COFFIN: Come on, that was nothing! Fake news! Pure gotcha journalism!

MITSY: Look sir, I don't know if you know how the media works these days, but you don't get to complain about "gotcha journalism" if the journalists actually get you!

COFFIN: Look, I can explain everything. It'll just take a while.

MITSY: Good! Because we're not letting you in front of a camera again until you make everything nice and sparkling clear! Maddie, what do you think?

MADDIE: Me? Oh I don't really care. All I know is you're gonna have to double whatever you're paying me to fix this. That's how bad this is! *(COFFIN, MITSY, & MADDIE exit.)*

SCENE 6: Offices of Citizens for Coffin Joe

*A political office space filled with posters, streamers, and balloons for **COFFIN JOE**. In addition, there is a large map of different political districts colored in red, blue, and gray (Republican, Democrat, Cemetery). **STAFFERS** work in the background as **ARI** sits at a table and **LUPINA** stands at cabinets leafing through files. Also at the table is **JOCELYN IMHOTEP**, a Cleopatra-styled mummy in a power suit. She smiles at an open laptop.*

JOCELYN: *(To laptop.)* Hello everybody, and welcome to the Citizens for Coffin Joe Townhall political livestream! I'll be taking all your questions live in the chat room. Remember to @ me and keep up with the #CoffinJoeForPresident. I'll be here all hour! *(To ARI.)* I'm sorry I couldn't reschedule this, Ari.

ARI: Oh, no. Sure. I don't mind. I run Joe's campaign. I'm used to being second banana to 24-hour internet addicts.

JOCELYN: Our first question is from SurrenderDorothy2-1-2 —it says, "What can you tell us about the District Reaper's position on the Wicked Witch community?" Well, Coffin Joe is a supporter of all religions, all faiths, especially Wicca!

ARI: Jocelyn, that question was about Wicked Witches, not Wicca! They're two completely different things!

JOCELYN: *(To ARI.)* Quiet, will you? Kansas is gonna be a swing state! Whatever this is about, can't it wait until I take a sponsor break?

ARI: Oh, sure, sure. It's not like we've got anything to worry about. Just our candidate about to be torpedoed by somebody new entering the race. No big deal.

JOCELYN: Oh, cry me a river. And I don't mean the Nile! *(To laptop.)* To SkullsSkullsAndMoreSkulls, yes! Coffin Joe does support legalizing piranha plants, but only for medical purposes. Now, let's see what our next question is... *(ARI gets frustrated, takes out his phone, and begins furiously typing on it.)*

JOCELYN: Ah, here's a new user on the livestream! Welcome to the chat, PoliticalPaladin_4-1-1! What a lovely name! PoliticalPaladin asks, "When are you going to answer my questions you conniving partisan hack. Just get off the computer and talk to me, look up from your laptop, yes this is me for goodness sake, I said look up from your laptop..." *(JOCELYN slows her reading, and looks up, then down, then up again. ARI waves at her. She rolls her eyes.)* Oh, look at that! It's time for a short break for our sponsor, SoulHack.com. Remember! If you want to take control of your own afterlife, the quickest and cheapest option is SoulHack.com! *(To ARI.)* PoliticalPaladin? Really?

ARI: What do you want? I do intramural D&D on the weekends.

JOCELYN: Okay, spill it, Ari. What do you want?

ARI: What do I want? I'm sorry. What do I want? Jocelyn! This isn't about what I want; it's about what our candidate wants!

JOCELYN: Ari, Ari! As Party Chairwoman, you know I'm committed to supporting our candidate. That doesn't mean I'm committed to letting you yell at me!

ARI: Okay, okay! I'm sorry! But I need an explanation about what's going on with his PAC looking for a new candidate.

JOCELYN: You know the rules, Ari. Legally speaking you can't talk to them, and neither can we. They're operating completely outside the party. I wash my hands of them.

LUPINA: Then...Why are the PAC's checks being routed to the same account as these offices, Miss Imogene?

JOCELYN: That's Imhotep! It's Egyptian! And who are you? *(To ARI.)* Who is she?

ARI: She's Lupina, and she's awesome! Answer the question!

JOCELYN: Fine. The rule says we can't communicate with any political action committee. But! There isn't anything in the rules that forbids us from making financial exchanges.

LUPINA: Really? That's interesting...

JOCELYN: Interesting? What's so interesting about it?

ARI: Oh, just wait. This is where she gets good.

LUPINA: You're saying you can pay the PAC as much money as you want. Is that right?

JOCELYN: Yes. What, do you want me to explain how the post office works next?

LUPINA: Well, I'm just a little confused because this file says that money is being withdrawn from PAC accounts and being funneled into your offices. Not the other way around, like you said.

JOCELYN: English, please?

ARI: It means we've got you, Josie. Hook, line and sinker.

JOCELYN: *(Sighing.)* Unless…?

LUPINA: Unless you tell us who this Dark Horse candidate is you're thinking of running against Coffin Joe.

JOCELYN: Sorry, but there's not much I can tell you… Plausible deniability, that's the key to winning in this business!

ARI: Right, so how did this work? You just took orders from above, handled the money side of it, and handed everything off to somebody else?

JOCELYN: More or less. I had my contact, they had their contact, and so on and so on.

ARI: Great. It's untraceable. It's like a giant game of telephone!

LUPINA: Hold on. Who were your contacts?

JOCELYN: Why? It doesn't matter. I don't know who they were talking to.

LUPINA: Yeah, but humor me. Who did you talk to?

JOCELYN: Well, above me there was Dante Shapiro in Abyss Management. He was the one who suggested we go with the Vampire angle. And below me there was… oh who was it… Victoria Talbot, Media.

ARI: *(Standing, hands up.)* Okay, okay! Let me think… Shapiro and Talbot…Shapiro and Talbot…

LUPINA: What are you thinking?

ARI: I'm thinking if I can figure out who Shapiro and Talbot's contacts were I can reverse-engineer this whole underground daisy-chain and figure out who they're running against Joe!

LUPINA: Right. Well, I'm getting a text from Mitsy, so I'd better take this. Can you take the rest of this from here?

ARI: Sure, sure! Don't distract me! *(LUPINA leaves. ARI paces while making motions in the air with his hands as though he's moving invisible pieces on a board in front of him.)* Alright…So Shapiro's in Abyss Management, which puts him in the same house as Richter and Simons in Acquisitions, who both own stock in Lockness Martin! And the CEO is Yeti Sasquin, naturally! All the Cryptids stick together!

JOCELYN: Look at you go, Ari! Right down the Rabbit Hole!

ARI: So, Yeti would talk to Abiyoyo, who's an honorary member of the Leprechaun Newscaster Society! The leprechaun vote is always a big X factor…But who would they want as candidate? Let's see, there's McGonnical, Macintosh, McTaggart…

JOCELYN: How about… MacGuffin?

ARI: MacGuffin, right! I forgot him! Wait, who's MacGuffin?

JOCELYN: Nobody. *(Louder.)* You hear me? MacGuffin! Now! *(Suddenly agents in white with little wings on their backs burst out, handcuffing ARI.)*

ARI: Why you…You dirty double-crossing sneak! You set me up! What are you wearing, a wire?

JOCELYN: Wearing a wire? No, no. I am the wire! And now, I've got you! Hook, line, and sinker!

ARI: You can't do this! You don't have any jurisdiction here! I want to talk to my lawyer! I have rights!

JOCELYN: Yeah, like the right to remain silent. I suggest you use it. Take him away! *(A blindfold is put over ARI's eyes, and he's dragged away, kicking, and screaming.)*

ACT II

SCENE 7: Witch's Brew in the AM

*Television studio set, somewhat like the 66 Minutes set, but with a cozy looking couch and coffee table, with cups of coffee served for everyone. A sign with a cup of coffee and a witch stirring it like a cauldron, reading Witch's Brew in the AM. A pair of yuppie looking witches and a black cat, **GLINDA**, **ELMYRA**, and **OMELAS**, sit on the couch in front of cameras laughing, fake sounding, as music leads them in from a commercial break. **CAMERA PERSON** stands manning a camera pointed at the couch.*

GLINDA: And we're back! Hey there to everyone just tuning in! This is *Witch's Brew in the AM*, and we're your cackling crones with the coffee, Glinda!

ELMYRA: And Elmyra! And of course, our very favorite familiar, Omelas!

OMELAS: Yes, and now that we're done with the commercials, we can talk about our main story—the Coffin Joe scandal machine!

GLINDA: Tell me about it! They're printing so many tabloids about his campaign. There's nothing left to wrap fish in!

ELMYRA: What about you, Omelas? Are you planning to vote for Coffin Joe?

OMELAS: Uh, considering I'm a cat, and I'm not legally allowed to vote? Probably not.

ELMYRA: Oh quiet. You're just mad they won't legalize catnip.

GLINDA: Our guests today are Coffin Joe himself, along with his senior campaign advisor Mitsy Morte! *(MITSY and COFFIN enter, the song "Don't Fear the Reaper" playing as their intro. They awkwardly sit down and smile.)*

GLINDA: So, Joe! Mitsy! Welcome to the show!

COFFIN: Happy to be here! Isn't that right Mitsy?

MITSY: If by "happy" you mean contractually obligated, then yes!

ELMYRA: Woah woah, slow down girl! Not all of us here have a law degree!

GLINDA: I do! I was a prosecutor for ten years before I went on the air.

ELMYRA: Oh, you were just lucky to be around for the Nixon post-death trials! They would've put anyone on the air to cover that!

OMELAS: Ladies, ladies! Ahem. *(All businesslike.)* Mr. District Reaper, your campaign has been plagued by a host of problems. First there was inflammatory rhetoric on the campaign trail. Then, there was the pay-for-play soul trafficking scandal, and now your chief of staff, Ari Westphal, has been indicted by the Heaven Security Administration. Is that about right? *(ELMYRA and GLINDA look at each other, amazed. MITSY and COFFIN do the same.)*

COFFIN: You're a cat.

OMELAS: Sir, please just answer the question.

MITSY: I'll take this. Look, we're not here to play gotcha journalism or answer leading questions designed to trap the candidate into saying the wrong thing...

OMELAS: You mean telling the truth?

MITSY: Whatever. I'll tell you what we are here for—to speak for the people of this great community, and everything it stands for! From the highest peaks of the Death Mountains, to the lowest graves in our cemeteries!

OMELAS: Speaking of that, Ms. Morte, care to comment at all about the recent allegations of voting zone redistricting that has effectively cut off nearly all graveyard residents from the next election?

MITSY: Uh... I'm sorry, what?

OMELAS: It's pretty simple. The voting map has been gerrymandered to cut the population of several key cemeteries out of their usual voting districts, and put them into new ones where they'll be outnumbered by the Necromancer demographic! And everyone knows that dead people and necromancers don't get along!

MITSY: They don't?

COFFIN: Look, let me make this simple for you, kitty cat. I don't care how much the voting map has changed or what kind of gerrymandering you want to talk about. Truth is, most of those so called cemetery residents shouldn't even be allowed to vote in our elections, period!

GLINDA: Really? Care to elaborate, Mr. Reaper?

COFFIN: It's like this. We've got people coming into our country from all over the world, and just because they happen to die here, they get full afterlife citizenship and voting rights in our elections! Now tell me, how is that a fair system?

MITSY: Oh no. He's doing it again...

COFFIN: After all, what about all of the monsters and paranormal citizens who were born and raised right here in this land? Born and raised and died in it? Or were summoned here from another dimension, or cobbled together from corpses in laboratories right here? What about their rights?

OMELAS: But sir, aren't we supposed to be a nation of immigrants?

ELMYRA: That's right! Our ancestors all got chased out of some country by villagers with torches and pitchforks! Do we really wanna do the same thing here?

GLINDA: Ooh! Good one, Elmyra!

ELMYRA: Spare me, Glinda. Oh wait, you meant it that time!

COFFIN: Look, all I'm saying is, if you wanna be able to cast a vote, you should at the very least be forced to produce an up-to-date driver's license to do so. And a birth certificate. And a death certificate, while you're at it! If you wanna vote, that's what I wanna know! Where's your death certificate?

ELMYRA: *(Fingers to her temples.)* And hold it, hold it... I'm getting a sign from the spirits... That it's time for our commercial break! Stay tuned and after this word from our sponsors, we'll ask Coffin Joe what he wears at home inside his coffin!

CAMERA PERSON: Aaaaaaand, we're clear!

ELMYRA: Finally! *(To COFFIN.)* Joe, beautiful work out there. The camera loves you! You're killing it!

GLINDA: Just don't flame out too quick, okay? Save that for sweeps. *(Everyone except MITSY and JOE exit, leaving them alone.)*

COFFIN: Well, this is going well, isn't it?

MITSY: Going well? Going well! This isn't going well! I'm going out of my mind. That's how it is going!

COFFIN: Relax, relax. Everything's gonna be okay.

MITSY: I don't get it! Every time I clear up one of your scandals, you just say something new that gets everything going again! It's like you have some sort of subconscious instinct to get the media foaming at the mouth! It's like you're trying to sabotage your own campaign!

COFFIN: Yes.

MITSY: I'm sorry, I'm a couple centuries old, so maybe my hearing is going. I thought you said you were trying to sabotage your campaign.

COFFIN: Yes, that's right. I am.

MITSY: *(Putting down her things.)* Will you excuse me, for a moment? I need to take care of something. *(She exits. She screams offstage. She re-enters, calm.)* There! That felt better!

COFFIN: Look, if you'll just let me explain; it'll all make sense.

MITSY: Oh, it makes sense, alright! A sick, twisted kind of sense! You don't want to win the election at all, do you? This is all just some sort of…publicity stunt!

COFFIN: More or less.

MITSY: What's going on? For real, I mean! If you want to lose so bad, why are you running in the first place?

COFFIN: Well, it's like you said. This will be great publicity when it's all done! Sure, I'll tank the campaign, but with my profile up, I'll be able to get what I really want… *(He leans in, whispering.)* A TV show!

MITSY: A TV show?

COFFIN: Sure! A TV show! One of the lawyer ones! I don't wanna be a politician, really. I wanna be an actor. Like... Ronald Reagan!

MITSY: No, but he's the other way around. He's an actor who became a politician.

COFFIN: He was? Okay, makes sense. He was always an inspiration to me. He gave me the idea for my whole "Trickle Down Heavenomics" plan!

MITSY: *(To herself.)* It'll be the closest he'll ever get to heaven, that's for sure...

COFFIN: Okay, then that other guy. Fred Dalton... what's his name. I can play District Attorney on TV!

MITSY: But you're already District Attorney in real life!

COFFIN: District REAPER. Nobody makes TV shows about them! *(Sudden thought.)* Hey, maybe I could pitch that! *Special Reapers Unit*! Whadya think?

MITSY: I think you'd be a lot better off just DOING YOUR JOB. You wanna be on TV? You're already on the news, 24/7!

COFFIN: Ah, c'mon! That's boring! Do you know how much time I have to waste sitting through one case after another? It's the same thing, over and over. All petty crimes. Nothing big and splashy! Nothing ripped from the headlines!

MITSY: You want ripped from the headlines? You are the headlines! Why'd you hire me to get rid of your scandals if you just want to make more of them?

COFFIN: Because you need to get rid of the old scandals if you want to make more happen! Otherwise people will just get bored of the same old stories, and they'll actually look at you, and your record! And you know what I'm afraid of?

MITSY: They'll actually elect you?

COFFIN: Exactly! And believe me, that's the last thing you want to happen! I mean, if I get bored there, there's no telling what I'll do! Heck, I'll call up aliens and have them blow up the Earth if someone cooks my steak wrong!

MITSY: Okay. Now that I know what the score is; I think I can help you drive this campaign into the ground like a professional.

COFFIN: Great!

MITSY: Oh, and my price is going up.

COFFIN: Don't push it.

MITSY: Try me. Or I'll get you elected for real.

COFFIN: You wouldn't!

PRODUCTION ASSISTANT 1 *(Enters.)*: Okay, everybody on set! *(ELMYRA, GLINDA, & OMELAS return along with CAMERA PERSON and PRODUCTION ASSISTANT 2. COFFIN fumes at MITSY.)*

ELMYRA: Okay, nobody get in the way of my lights! I want them to get my good side!

GLINDA: You don't have a good side. You just put a charm on camera B.

ELMYRA: Well, cheaper than a face lift. But then, you wouldn't know about that, would you, Glinda?

OMELAS: Can you please get this out of your system before we go live? We don't want another one of your quibs on YouTube…

MITSY: *(Whispering.)* Well, how about it, Joe? Either I blab your plan to the world, or you tack another couple zeroes onto my paycheck.

COFFIN: *(Whispering.)* You're the worst, you know that? The worst!

MITSY: *(Whispering.)* Of course I am! I'm Mitsy Morte! That's why you hired me.

PRODUCTION ASSISTANT 2: And we're live in five, four, three, two…

COFFIN: *(Whispering.)* Fine, fine! Just play along!

ELMYRA: And we're back! Elmyra and Glinda here again with our guest, Mr. Coffin Joe. Next up, we're going to ask the candidate what he thinks about the vote to tear down historic monuments of Vampire Generals from the Civil War!

OMELAS: I can't imagine you have anything controversial to say about that, do you, Joe? *(COFFIN JOE and MITSY smile awkwardly.)*

MITSY: Angels and ministers of grace defend us…

SCENE 8: An Undisclosed Location

*A mysterious black room, all the windows taped up with newspapers to obscure the view. **ARI** sits handcuffed in a chair with a blindfold over his eyes, flanked by several **ANGELS** in suits and sunglasses, their wings sticking out. The opera section from "Bohemian Rhapsody" plays. A long pause.*

ARI: Uh, excuse me?

ANGEL 1: Shh.

ARI: Look, I was scared at first, but now I'm just confused. What's going on here?

ANGEL 2: Quiet! We're the ones who ask the questions!

ARI: Well, are you going to ask me any questions? Or are you just going to keep playing that song over and over again? I want to talk to my attorney! I have rights!

ANGEL 1: Attorney's for a court of law. You're waaaaaaay out of that jurisdiction, pal.

ANGEL 2: Yeah, we answer to a higher authority!

ARI: Meaning what? You work for a giant hot dog or something?

ANGEL 1: You better not keep giving us lip, buddy.

ANGEL 2: Yeah. Or else.

ARI: Or else what? *(The **ANGELS** look at each other. The tape runs out. **ANGEL 1** picks up the boombox, rewinds the tape, and plays it again, from the beginning.)*

ARI: Okay, I changed my mind. I don't want you to torture me.

ANGEL 1: Oh yeah?

ARI: Yeah, if you're gonna keep playing that song I think I'd like to skip right ahead to execution.

CLARENCE: *(Offstage.)* Are you kidding? What's going on here?

JOCELYN: *(Offstage.)* Please, sir. We're in the middle of things right now! *(CLARENCE ODDBODY, senior angel with a pocket watch, bursts in, followed by JOCELYN.)*

CLARENCE: In the middle of things? You mind telling me what this is?

JOCELYN: Please, Mr. Oddbody. We're just interrogating the subject—

CLARENCE: Interrogating? All I've heard out of this room the past few minutes has been music! Who are you questioning, a jukebox?

JOCELYN: It's psychological tactics, sir! He'll crack sooner or later!

ARI: No, I won't. Only thing this is doing is making me want to cancel my iTunes membership.

JOCELYN: Well, he would have broken by now if you would let us use some of the old methods...

CLARENCE: Alright, alright, that's enough! We don't do the whole fire and brimstone "shock and awe" thing anymore! *(JOCELYN grumbles, and pulls the blindfold off ARI's head. He looks around, in a panic.)*

ARI: Wings? I knew it! You goons are with the Halo Squad!

CLARENCE: Please, please. Forgive my associates, Mr. Westphal, they may have treated you a little harshly.

ARI: A little harshly? This is unjust! This is illegal! And it's probably bad for my sciatica, too!

CLARENCE: The name's Clarence Oddboddy, Angel First Class, Intelligence Division.

ARI: Good, remind me to write that down so I know exactly who to get fired once I get out of... Where are we, exactly?

CLARENCE: Let's just call it an Undisclosed Location. I bet you've already figured out why you're here, haven't you?

ARI: I have an idea... Something to do with Coffin Joe, right?

CLARENCE: We certainly didn't bring you up here to look at the view, did we?

ARI: Ha ha. Look, I'm not gonna rat on the District Reaper, or turn state's evidence, or anything. I've been in this business a long time, and believe it or not, I still believe in a little thing called loyalty.

CLARENCE: Loyalty, huh? That's very commendable, Mr. Westphal. I wish I had a few people like you on my staff. Everybody here wants a promotion up to Archangel.

ANGEL 1: I'd settle for more vacation time.

ANGEL 2: A pension would be nice.

CLARENCE: See what I mean? But no, you believe in loyalty. That's good. That's a good thing to have in this day and age. Shame it isn't being returned…

ARI: Oh, come on! This is amateurish! You're just trying to make me suspicious of Coffin Joe, aren't you?

CLARENCE: See, what'd I tell you? Our friend here isn't stupid enough to fall for our tricks.

ARI: That's right! But… Just out of curiosity… Just how exactly were you planning to fool me?

CLARENCE: Well… It's all a little complicated…

ARI: Go ahead! Try me! You know I'm clever!

CLARENCE: Good man! Jocelyn, bring in the big board. *(She nods, not complaining, and brings in a board from offstage. It's full of pictures, names, articles, and documents put up with thumbtacks wrapped with thread connecting different things. Classic conspiracy board. CLARENCE stands up and points.)*

ARI: Oh boy.

CLARENCE: Now. When Coffin Joe's campaign began six months ago, you started running a fifty million dollar ad campaign on tv, radio, the web. Fifty million is a lot of money, so we did a little digging to find out where it came from.

ARI: Well don't ask me, because honest to goodness, I really don't know. I have to remain in the dark as much as possible—

CLARENCE: We know, we know… plausible deniability. But that doesn't even matter to us. You know why?

ARI: Enlighten me.

CLARENCE: Because the fifty million dollars we traced into the campaign's accounts was dated a year ago, not just six months.

ARI: Wait… A year ago…?

CLARENCE: Tax records, from a Transylvanian Bank account. Paid in deposits of gold bullion from unknown origins. Most of it's been redacted, but you can see the bank wires were handled 12 months ago to the day!

ARI: That's before I even joined the campaign…! But…but it's no big deal. After all, big donors try and donate to recruit candidates all the time.

CLARENCE: Sure, but who are the big donors? Who wanted Coffin Joe for President?

ARI: Okay, fine. So he's got his issues. Sometimes it feels like my entire job is just cleaning the trail of destruction in his wake!

CLARENCE: Exactly! Destruction! Look at all the reports of bad omens this election cycle! Statues screaming! Earthquakes around the world! And a cow giving birth to a calf with three heads that shoot lasers out of their eyes!

ARI: Okay, okay! But that doesn't tell you who's paying for him.

CLARENCE: Yes it does! Somebody who wants destruction, that's who!

ARI: I can't think of anybody in the world who'd want that!

CLARENCE: Exactly! Because it isn't anybody in the world. (*CLARENCE points to the board and turns it over. It has pictures of UFOs and aliens on it.*)

ARI: (*Sighing.*) Aliens…? Really…? I can't believe I'm saying this out loud…

CLARENCE: Look who you're talking to, bud. Most people don't even believe in the U.S.

ARI: You really think that aliens want to elect a President to destroy the world?

CLARENCE: Sure! Why not get us to do the job for them?

ARI: But how could they pay him fifty million for his campaign? What, are they paying him in space dollars?

CLARENCE: No, it's the unknown gold bullion! The Transylvanian Bank that received the gold had to be evacuated when it turned out the gold was radioactive! If it's too radioactive for vampires, it has to be aliens!

ARI: I don't know what to say...

CLARENCE: That's alright. We just need you to agree to work with us. Help us find out what's really going on here!

ARI: I told you; I don't know anything!

CLARENCE: No, but Coffin Joe does. And if you can get him to talk...

ARI: Talk? Wait, you want me to wear a wire? No way!

CLARENCE: Mr. Westphal, please, it's the only way to find out!

ARI: Yeah, and it's the only way to make sure I'm dead in this business! If word gets out that I sold out a client and worked with you guys, I'll never work again!

CLARENCE: Sure, and if the world gets destroyed, you'll have job offers lined up around the block, right?

ARI: Hey, I'm in crisis management. It might be good for my business if there's an apocalypse!

CLARENCE: Mr. Westphal, you're leaving me with no other choice...

ARI: Yeah, go on. You don't scare me. I can see through all your tricks, remember? This good cop, bad cop stuff won't work on me.

CLARENCE: Oh yeah? How about...good cop, weird cop?

ARI: Weird cop? What's that supposed to mean?

CLARENCE: *(To JOCELYN.)* Send him to the Red Room.

ARI: The Red Room? The Red Room! Hey, wait a minute!

CLARENCE: Ah, you've heard of it?

ARI: I thought the Red Room was just a myth! It doesn't exist!

CLARENCE: Well, on paper, it doesn't. But sometimes our people like to get a little creative and go off script.

ARI: You can't do this! You can't send me there!

JOCELYN: Oh yeah? Watch me! *(To **CLARENCE**.)* Uh, can we?

CLARENCE: Of course we can! Nothing to worry about. After all, why worry about being sent to a place that doesn't exist? *(**JOCELYN** pulls **ARI** away on the chair, as he screams.)*

SCENE 9: Courtroom

*Hardwood paneled courtroom with a big podium for the judge in the center, flags and an emblem behind him reading "In God We Trust." **MITSY** and **MADDIE** sit at a table on one side of the courtroom. On the other sits **DEWEY**, **CHESTER**, and **HOWE** at the other, alongside **MEPHISTO** and **MARCATO**. A **GUARD** also stands by the court podium.*

MADDIE: Okay, so let me get this straight… He doesn't want to win? Why not just quit running in the first place?

MITSY: I dunno. He's kinda all over the place. Money? Ego? Ugh, I'm sorry I got you dragged into this.

MADDIE: No, don't be sorry! I'm totally cool with a fake presidential run as long as we all get paid!

MITSY: At the rate this is going, I'll be happy as long as we don't all wind up in prison.

MADDIE: Oh, that reminds me. What are they suing us for again?

MITSY: Ah… Y'know, I don't even know anymore? I lost track somewhere around when Joe started talking about aliens.

MADDIE: Oh yeah, aliens! Which type did he mean, exactly?

MITSY: Which type? You mean there's different types?

MADDIE: There's the Martians, the Grays, the Bigfoots… *(MITSY gives her a weird look.)* Oh yeah, Bigfoots are aliens, according to Joe. And they're hoarding the world's supply of Rogaine, or something.

MITSY: Maddie, Maddie, please. I had nightmares about this case last night, and I still don't remember what it is! *(To CHEATAM.)* Hey, Chester!

CHESTER: Can it wait, Mitsy? I'm a little busy at the moment.

MITSY: Remind me, is this the Voter Fraud case, or the Campaign Finance one? There's just so many lawsuits nowadays I can't keep track of them all.

CHESTER: Don't worry, Mitsy, it'll all be over soon and you can get back to doing your pro-bono defense stuff, or whatever it is you do.

HOWE: Ha! That's a good one! When we're done with her she'll be lucky to get a job as a prison lawyer doing ten to twenty!

DEWEY: Howard, this isn't a criminal case. We're suing her for compensatory damages.

HOWE: Compensatory? Diana, do I look like a dictionary?

MEPHISTO: She means money, you blockhead!

MARCATO: Yeah! We want to get her money, not send her to prison!

MITSY: *(To MADDIE.)* Good! We finally learned something!

MADDIE: Learned what? There's too many lawsuits to keep track of! How is that supposed to help us?

MITSY: Trust me, Maddie, I don't need to know what the case IS. As long as I know it's about money, I know how to beat them!

GUARD: All rise! *(Everybody stands. JUDGE ABERNATHY, a grumpy looking dragon enters.)* The Honorable Judge Firebrand Abernathy presiding!

MADDIE: Uh oh, it's Abernathy! He hates us!

MITSY: Eh, it's not so bad. He hates everybody!

ABERNATHY: Alright! Sit down and shut up! *(They all sit.)* Okay, what kind of nonsense have you brought to my courtroom today? *(The GUARD hands him a file.)* Seems pretty open and shut to me. How does the defense plead?

MITSY: Uh… We plead… *(Whispering.)* What do we plead?

MADDIE: *(Whispering.)* Don't ask me! Go with your gut!

MITSY: Uh… Not guilty by reason of insanity!

MADDIE. *(Under her breath to MITSY)*: Insanity? Really?

MITSY. *(Under her breath to MADDIE)*: Well, it is Coffin Joe we're talking about.

ABERNATHY: *(Banging gavel.)* Order! Order in the court! That means shut up! So what do the plaintiffs say? *(Nervous silence.)* That means you idiots, at the other table! You got a settlement offer, or what? I'm supposed to be playing golf today!

DEWEY: Well, you have my sympathies, Your Honor. Perhaps if the defense would be willing to save everybody's time and render a plea of "guilty"…

MITSY: Yeah. And maybe you'd like to stop wasting all our time and throw away the dozen other lawsuits you've hit my client with since we beat your butts!

ABERNATHY: A dozen other lawsuits! Am I gonna have to hear evidence on all these cases?

MADDIE: Well, we can't very well let all these charges go unsubstantiated, Your Honor…

CHESTER: Hold on, hold on! Your Honor, they can't do this! Those cases are in completely different courts! We don't need to waste your time with this!

ABERNATHY: Are you saying those other dozen cases are a waste of time?

CHESTER: Well… Uh… Not exactly…

ABERNATHY: Because I'll be happy to dismiss all the charges you've brought against the defense if it means I make it to my Country Club!

MITSY: Excuse me, Your Honor, I'm still waiting on whether you'll allow my insanity plea?

DEWEY: Her client can't plead insanity, Your Honor! He's already pleaded not guilty to all the other cases. Why didn't he trot out this defense before?

MITSY: Does that mean you're opening the door to allowing all the other cases be read here in court?

CHESTER: No! No, of course not! We're just saying there's already been a precedent set in the previous cases as to… uh… Help me out here, guys!

HOWE: As to your client's state of mind. In other words… *(To DEWEY.)* Your turn!

DEWEY: In other words, insanity is a legal term for determining criminal culpability, not financial liability! *(Catching breath.)* Phew!

MITSY: You're forgetting, Diana, there's already case precedent for this! Jekyll Vs. Hyde!

DEWEY: That case doesn't apply here! Jekyll and Hyde were the same person! He was suing himself!

MITSY: Exactly! An insanity plea is admissible if the case itself is insane!

ABERNATHY: It's driving me crazy; that's for sure...

DEWEY: Fine! If she wants to use an insanity plea, go ahead! But that means you're throwing out your previous defense.

CHESTER: That's right! Fruit of the poisonous tree!

HOWE: And it means your client will be liable on all those other charges again! Unless you want to convince a dozen other judges that Coffin Joe is crazy!

MITSY: Actually, no. It won't be a dozen other judges. Just him.

HOWE: What?

ABERNATHY. *(Outraged)*: What?

MITSY: Oh, don't you see? You're the presiding judge! You'll be hearing every single case they have against us!

ABERNATHY: Are you kidding me?

MADDIE: Sorry, Judge. They're not leaving us a whole lot of wiggle room here.

ABERNATHY: Plaintiffs, am I getting this right? You're playing hardball with the defense and willing to drag in a dozen more cases that I'll have to deal with in here, all over this case? A parking ticket?

MITSY: Parking ticket! I knew I missed something!

MEPHISTO: Hey! That parking ticket is no laughing matter!

MARCATO: Coffin Joe parked his campaign bus in a red zone on his last stop! Red zones are only for handicapped demons!

ABERNATHY: A parking ticket!

DEWEY: Your Honor, please! If we get this case, we'll be able to open all kinds of evidence that could bring Coffin Joe down! Bribery, racketeering… There may even be wire-taps from the Heaven Security Administration in his bus that we can—

ABERNATHY: Oh no! I'm not letting you turn this into a fishing expedition! Exactly how mad do you want to make me Miss… What's your name again?

DEWEY: Diana Dewey, Your Honor. Of the firm of Dewey…

CHESTER: Cheatam…

HOWE: And—

ABERNATHY: Stop right there! If you say "And Howe" I will personally hold you in contempt of court! You got that?

HOWE: But… But it's my name!

ABERNATHY: I don't care what your name is! I've got a strict "No Puns Allowed" rule in my courtroom, especially for an ancient gag like that! Now, what were you saying? *(DEWEY looks at her partners, and nods.)*

DEWEY: Diana Dewey, Your Honor. Of the firm of Dewey…

CHESTER: Cheatam…

HOWE: And Howe!

ABERNATHY: Guard! Lock him up!

DEWEY: You'll have to lock us all up, Your Honor!

CHESTER: Yeah! Nobody messes with our firm!

ABERNATHY: Fine! Lock them all up! I'm tired of even looking at you bums! *(The GUARD drags them away in handcuffs. MEPHISTO and MARCATO sit dumbfounded.)*

MEPHISTO: What just happened here?

MARCATO: I knew I shouldn't have sold my soul again to cover the legal fees!

MITSY: Your Honor, in light of the plaintiff's counsel being… um… arrested… I move that—

ABERNATHY: Alright, alright! Shut up! I'm finding this case in favor of the defense and throwing it out with prejudice! *(Bangs gavel.)* Case dismissed! Now outta my way, I've got a tee-time to make! *(ABERNATHY exits. LUPINA enters.)*

MITSY: Lupina! Good news! We won the case!

LUPINA: Great. Uh… What case?

MITSY: Oh, who cares. Where've you been? I've been trying to reach you all day!

LUPINA: It's Ari! I lost track of him after our meeting with the Party Chairwoman, and I haven't been able to get him on his cell phone either. It's like he disappeared off the face of the earth.

MITSY: Hmm. That's weird. Maybe he just got fed up and split. It'd make sense for somebody on this campaign to go insane.

MADDIE: This Party Chairwoman he was seeing. What was her name?

LUPINA: I think it was Jocelyn something. Jocelyn Imhotep.

MADDIE: Wait! Wait! Wait! I think I'm getting an idea! Nobody say anything. It'll only distract me! *(At her snakes.)* That goes double for all you with the hissing! Zip it! *(MADDIE pauses, her hands up, making faces like she's almost about to say something or sneeze.)*

LUPINA: Should we get a doctor?

MITSY: Shh! This is good!

MADDIE: *(Snapping.)* I've got it! Jocelyn Imhotep! Of the Egyptian Imhoteps! Her family cornered the market on mummification and afterlife services back before the rise of the Roman Empire. She's not just some Party Chairwoman! She's in deep with the Heaven Security Administration!

MITSY: The HSA? Seriously?

MADDIE: Of course! It all makes sense! Coffin Joe's been under investigation by the Secret Angel crowd! And Dewey just mentioned the HSA. I'll bet anything they're in cahoots!

MITSY: You mean Dewey, Cheatam, and Howe are working with Angels and Devils?

MADDIE: Why not? They're lawyers!

MITSY: Good point.

LUPINA: If that's the case, then what happened to Ari?

MADDIE: Well, they've got a lot of undisclosed locations, but if they really wanted to keep him out of sight, they'd take him to the Red Room.

LUPINA: The Red Room... I've heard of it... They say it can drive people insane... And almost nobody gets out...

MITSY: Well, you know what this means.

MADDIE: What?

MITSY: It means Coffin Joe's gonna need a new chief of staff. We're gonna get promotions, for sure!

LUPINA: But what about Ari?

MITSY: Oh c'mon. He's a professional. Them's the breaks.

LUPINA: Not if I have anything to say about it! *(She leaves.)*

MITSY: Wait! Where are you going?

LUPINA. *(Offstage)*: What does it look like? I'm gonna get lost! *(MITSY exits.)*

SCENE 10: The Red Room

A surreal landscape – A set of waiting room chairs sitting in front of a backdrop of Escher staircases. There are signs in a typical EXIT design on either side of the stage that read NO EXIT.

*Several pictures hanging up—one of a highway, one of trees, one of coffee, and one of a smiling girl. Several people sit in chairs by coffee tables—a woman with **BLUE HAIR** carrying a log, a man in a **BOW TIE** drinking coffee, and a person wearing a **BIRD MASK**. The zig-zag wall opens, and **ARI** walks in. A loud laugh track plays.*

ARI: Uh… Hello? Where am I…? *(Laugh track.)* Ah! Where's that laughing coming from? *(Laugh track plays. **ARI** looks around and at the people behind him.)* You guys! Tell me, what is this place? What's going on here? And why are they playing the same darn laugh over and over again? Hello! *(Laugh track plays. None of the people in the room move. **ARI** waves his hand in front of their faces. They're still as mannequins.)* I gotta get out of here! *(**ARI** runs off stage. From the opposite end of the stage, his **DOPPELGANGER** appears, and looks around wildly. Laugh track plays.)*

DOPPELGANGER: I gotta get out of here! *(**DOPPELGANGER** runs off stage again, and **ARI** comes in from the other side, looking around wildly.)*

ARI: I gotta get out of here! Man, I'm getting déjà vu! *(**ARI** motions to run off, but **DOPPELGANGER** runs in from the same side that he just came in and bumps into him.)*

DOPPELGANGER: Ah! I'm sorry!

ARI: What? Nah, don't worry about it.

DOPPELGANGER: Thanks. I gotta get out of here!

ARI: You can say that again! *(Both of them freeze, and look at each other. They look like they're about to scream, but they're frozen stiff, and just circle one another on stage. They begin to gesticulate wildly, their motions matching exactly.)*

BOTH: I gotta get out of here…! *(Angry.)* Stop copying me! *(Angry.)* I'm not copying you; you're copying me! *(Confused.)* Or wait, am I…? *(Sitting down.)* I'm getting dizzy… I think I'm going to faint…! *(Both of them begin to fall down, but ARI bumps into DOPPELGANGER as he faints, and knocks DOPPELGANGER out of his trance. DOPPELGANGER catches ARI in his arms.)*

DOPPELGANGER: Ugh! I never realized I was so heavy…! Let's see… if I was unconscious, how would I wake myself up… Oh, I got it! Franklin Delano Roosevelt came back from the dead and he's running for President again, and he wants you to run his campaign!

ARI: *(Springing to life.)* Yes sir, Mister President, sir! *(Confused.)* Wait, what?

DOPPELGANGER: Okay, I know this is weird, but you gotta get it together…

ARI: Get it together? Get it together! Look at me! I'm trapped in a parallel dimension talking to my evil twin!

DOPPELGANGER: Hey! I'm not an evil twin!

ARI: Oh yeah? Prove it!

DOPPELGANGER: If I was an evil twin, I'd have a goatee!

ARI: *(Pause.)* You're right! How come I didn't know that? I'm losing my mind! I always knew this job would drive me crazy!

DOPPELGANGER: C'mon, c'mon! You're not crazy! There has to be a perfectly logical explanation for all of this!

MAGICIAN: *(Offstage.)* LOGIC? *(**ARI** and **DOPPELGANGER** back away as a **MAGICIAN** wearing a stage cape, tux, and carrying a wand appears, dramatically.)*

MAGICIAN: There is no logic… In the Red Room! *(The people behind them begin to go "oooooo" spookily.)*

DOPPELGANGER: Oh man, it's starting to get weird!

ARI: "Starting to?"

MAGICIAN: *(To the audience, not seeming to notice **ARI** and **DOPPELGANGER**.)* In the Red Room, there is no such thing as reality! Or common sense! There is only… illusion!

ARI: Illusion. He's talking about you.

DOPPELGANGER: Oh come on, now you're just being rude!

MAGICIAN: If we want to make lightning appear, we make thunder! *(MAGICIAN motions with his wand, and a stagey thunder rumbling comes from sheet sounds.)* If we want someone to answer a door, we hear a knock! *(He motions, and a knock-on-wood sound comes from offstage.)* And if we want to bend the laws of time and space, they bend! *(A sound from one of those plastic singing sound tube plays. ARI and DOPPELGANGER are freaked out.)*

DOPPELGANGER: Ah! We're doomed!

ARI: Time and space? Wait a minute! *(ARI goes off stage, and pulls a SOUND TECHNICIAN onto the stage carrying all the sound props, including the sound tube.)*

SOUND TECH: Yeesh! I don't get paid enough for this!

ARI: Relax, he's not breaking the laws of physics! It's just a bunch of special effects.

MAGICIAN: Exactly! That's all the world is, after all. A bunch of special effects. I am an expert in the art of suspension of disbelief! For that is the only thing that keeps any of us from going insane!

ARI: Yeah, whatever. If you're trying to scare me, it ain't working!

DOPPELGANGER: Speak for yourself!

ARI: I AM speaking for yourself! *(Confused.)* Myself! You know what I mean! Point is, I know exactly what's going on here!

DOPPELGANGER: That makes one of us!

ARI: Look, it's standard psychological torture! They have us kidnapped and brought us in for interrogation, but first they gotta break us! That's why they threw us in the Red Room!

DOPPELGANGER: Yeah! That's what they did to us! Wait, does that mean you don't think I'm just an evil doppelganger anymore?

ARI: I'm working on one mind bender at a time, man. I'll figure out what I think about you when I'm not stuck in crazy town anymore.

MAGICIAN: You aren't going anywhere, my friend! There is nowhere to go! We are everywhere and nowhere at once!

ARI: Oh please! If this is supposed to make me go insane, spare me. I work in politics. You have to be insane already to work there!

MAGICIAN: I warn you. Don't underestimate my powers! We are masters of time and space, especially time...

DOPPELGANGER: If you're a master of time could you speed up this little speech of yours?

MAGICIAN: Of course! But I can also slow it down!

(The MAGICIAN *waves his wand and* ARI *and* DOPPELGANGER *begin to move in slow motion. They reach out at the* MAGICIAN, *then look at each other horrified, trying to speak but not making any sense.*)

ARI: Whaaaaaaaaaaaaaaaaaaaaat iiiiiiiiiiiiiiiiiiiiiiiiiiiiiis haaaaaaaaaaaaaaaaaaapeeeeeeeeeeeeeeeeeeenniiiiiiiiiiiiiiiiiiiiiiiiiiiiiing?

DOPPELGANGER: IIIIIIIIIIIIIIIIIIIIIIIIIIIIIII feeeeeeeeeeeeeeeeeeel siiiiiiiiiiiiiiiiiiiiiiiiiiiiiiiiick!

ARI: Puuuuuuuuuuuuuuuuuuuuut yooooooooooooooooooour heeeeeeeeeeeeeeead beeeeeeeeeeeeeeeetweeeeeeeeeeeeeeen yoooooooooooooooour kneeeeeeeeeeeeeeeeeees...

DOPPELGANGER: Ooooooooooooookaaaaaaaaaaaaaaaay... (DOPPELGANGER *slowly bends down, but then winds up at the* MAGICIAN *for a punch.*) Haaaaaaaaaaaaaaaahaaaaaaaaaaaaaaahaaaaaaaaaaaa... IIIIIIIIIIIIIIIIIIII foooooooled yoooooooooooooooou!!!

ARI: Woooooooooooooooooooah! Goooooooooooooood oooooooooooooooooooone!

MAGICIAN: Haha, you fool! Like I told you, I'm a master of time and space! (*The* MAGICIAN *laughs, and ducks from* DOPPELGANGER'S *punches, blocking each one easily.*)

DOPPELGANGER: Uuuuuuuuuuuuuuuh ooooooooooooh...

ARI: IIIIIIIIIIIIIIIIIIIIIIIII kneeeeeeeeeeeew iiiiiiiiiiiiiiiiiiiiiiit waaaaaaaaaaaaaaaas aaaaaaaaaaaaaaaa baaaaaaaaaaaaaaaaad ideeeeeeeeeeeea...

DOPPELGANGER: Heeeeeeeeeeeeeey! Nooooooooooooooot coooooooooooooooool, maaaaaaaaaaaaaaaan!

MAGICIAN: You should've known better than to fight with me! Especially now! The Red Room is at its full power during the full moon! (*As they speak, the Escher staircases begin to rattle, and then slide open. LUPINA walks in, in full werewolf mode, wearing sunglasses and carrying her bent baseball bat. The MAGICIAN drops his wand and ARI and DOPPELGANGER return to normal.)*

MAGICIAN: Ah! What in the blazes!

DOPPELGANGER: Aaaaah! Everything's back to normal! Well, as normal as it gets here, I guess.

LUPINA. *(Confused)*: Uh... Do you want to explain what's going on here?

ARI: Oh! Uh...Not really.

LUPINA: Works for me.

MAGICIAN: Now just hold on here! I don't know who you are, but I don't allow anyone to just barge in on my pocket dimensions without permission!

LUPINA: Permission? I live my whole life without permission. I'm taking my friend back with me. Both of them!

DOPPELGANGER: Hey, I get to leave, too? Far out!

MAGICIAN: In your dreams! We have them on divine authority to meddle with their minds for the rest of time! Just who do you think you are, anyway?

LUPINA: *(Takes off her sunglasses.)* I'm Lupina. And I'm awesome. *(The MAGICIAN freezes, and all the people in the room behind them look at each other. Then they all run for the zig zag door.)*

MAGICIAN: Out of my way! I'm the one in charge; me first! *(Looking back at them.)* Sorry, Lupina, nothing personal! *(LUPINA spins her bat in her hand.)* Alright, alright! I'm going, I'm going! *(They leave. LUPINA, ARI, and DOPPELGANGER are left alone. ARI screams in relief.)*

ARI: Okay! First thing when we get back, I am charging Coffin Joe extra for all of that! *(Motions wildly.)*

LUPINA: Yeah, well. We've got a lot to talk about Coffin Joe on the way back. C'mon.

ARI: Woah, woah, woah! Wait just one second! I'm not going anywhere until you explain one thing! Did you do something different with your hair?

LUPINA: Oh, this. Well, y'know. It's a full moon. I'm a werewolf. Automatic bad hair day.

ARI: Don't say that! I think you look pretty good!

LUPINA: Eh, you're just saying that.

ARI: No, seriously! I wouldn't lie about that sort of thing! *(To DOPPELGANGER.)* Would I?

DOPPELGANGER: Don't ask me; I only just met you.

LUPINA: Oh yeah? What do you think, then?

DOPPELGANGER: I'm more into girls with pixie cuts, myself.

LUPINA: Okay, whatever. We better split now so we can get back in town before the election is over.

ARI: Oh, right! The election! Do you think we'll get there in time?

LUPINA: We will if I drive! Good thing there's no speed limits on Lost Highway!

DOPPELGANGER: Alright, let's get out of here. But wait, how did you get here, anyway?

LUPINA: Oh, that's easy. "You open this door with the key of imagination." *(They open the Escher staircases and exit to the "Twilight Zone" theme song.)*

SCENE 11: The Debate/The Election/ The Ending, Finally

The debate stage, two podiums on either end of an anchor table, in red, white & blue color scheme modeled after Presidential Debate soundstages. **OMELAS**, **GLINDA**, *and* **ELMYRA** *sit at the anchor table, to the audience.*

GLINDA: And we're minutes away from the big show! It's the most exciting night of the political season! That's right ladies and gentlemen, it's the Debate!

ELMYRA: It's also Election Night! People have been lined up since morning to vote for Coffin Joe, or the Dark Horse candidate! And we don't even know who that is!

GLINDA: Sure has been a wild and crazy election, hasn't it, Omelas?

OMELAS: If by wild and crazy you mean full of corruption, scandal, and brainwashed news coverage, then sure. What a ride! *(MITSY walks on stage, phone in her hand, followed by MADDIE.)*

MITSY: So Lupina's on her way with Ari. Hopefully he'll know what to do…

MADDIE: Okay, let's make a list of pros and cons. Let's say Coffin Joe wins. Pro?

MITSY: Pro! We just got… somebody… elected president!

MADDIE: And Con?

MITSY: He's insane! Insane! He'll start a war with Saturn just to keep from getting bored! Okay, so let's say he loses the election. Pro?

MADDIE: The world won't be destroyed. But con—our careers will be destroyed.

MITSY: Okay. So what would we rather be—dead, or unemployed?

MADDIE: That's not a fair comparison.

MITSY: Life ain't fair, baby. And neither are elections. *(MITSY's phone buzzes, and she picks up.)* Lupina, is that you? If you don't get here soon, so help me--

LUPINA: *(Offstage.)*: Relax, we're almost there! I can already hear you!

MITSY: Quit stalling, then! And turn down the volume on your phone. It's like I'm hearing double! *(LUPINA, ARI, and DOPPELGANGER show up.)*

ARI: Well don't blame me if we got here late! This one wanted to buy a newspaper!

DOPPELGANGER: Hey, don't get mad at me for that! The comic strips are all different in my dimension! I heard "Bloom County" is back in your world!

MITSY: Will both of you zip it! *(MITSY looks at them. She counts the **two ARIs**. She sighs.)* Let me guess. Doppelganger?

ARI and **DOPPELGANGER:** Uh-huh.

MITSY: *(Going up to **DOPPELGANGER**.)* Great. Okay, look, Ari—

LUPINA: No, the other one.

MITSY: *(Going up to **ARI**.)* Ari, I don't care where you were or what kind of... mystical mumbo jumbo! But we're in a big mess, and you've gotta fix it!

ARI: Yeah, that's nice. I quit.

MITSY: You what?

ARI: You heard me! I quit! I'm done being a political pawn! You, Coffin Joe, you're all the same! You use people left and right, and you throw them away!

MITSY: Hey, I'm a professional! Same as you!

ARI: Professional? You didn't lift a finger to help me, and neither did Coffin Joe! Lupina's the only one who cared enough to come save me from that nightmare!

LUPINA: He has been under a lot of stress, Mitsy.

MITSY: Oh, don't tell me you're taking his side, Lupina.

LUPINA: Hey, a lot's happened since I got him out from the Red Room. He's seen me after a full moon, and he doesn't mind that I shed.

MITSY: Ay caramba… How am I supposed to do this all on my own…?

DOPPELGANGER: Uh, Mitsy? You've still got me…

MITSY: I do? (Pause.) That's right. I do! Oh, thank God for doppelgangers! Okay, so, what've you got?

DOPPELGANGER: I've got the basics. Coffin Joe wins, the world ends. He loses, your career ends. So, hear me out… What if we just… Let Coffin Joe BE Coffin Joe?

ELMYRA: Viewers, this just in! Coffin Joe is in the building! Repeat, Coffin Joe is in the building! (COFFIN enters.)

COFFIN: Alright, Ari. Everything set up for the debate?

ARI: (Pointing in his face.) Yeah, you wanna hear it? I hope you lose the election! Not only that - I hope you get indicted on tax fraud! And soul trafficking! And collusion with aliens! And whatever else you did that I can't think of!

COFFIN: (To MITSY.) Did I miss something?

MITSY and LUPINA: No, the other one.

DOPPELGANGER: (Brushing off Joe's suit, making him look good.) There you are, Joe! Change of plans. Forget the prep, just be yourself. Say whatever you want!

COFFIN: Alright! That's more like it! (He runs to the podium.)

ARI: Did he even notice that there's suddenly two of us?

LUPINA: You're assuming he actually thinks about other people.

MITSY: Ari! Are you out of your mind?

DOPPELGANGER: It's perfect! Don't you see? If we let him go off-script, he's bound to say or do something so completely insane that it gets everyone too mad to vote for him! And when they ask us, we can just say—"It's not our fault! He went off script!"

MITSY: My god. You're right! It's genius!

MADDIE: But what if people actually like all the crazy stuff he winds up saying?

DOPPELGANGER: Oh c'mon. Nobody would ever fall for a huckster like him, would they?

ARI: You haven't been in this dimension very long, have you?

ELMYRA: And it's time for the show! Coffin Joe is here, and we're almost ready for the debate to begin! I'm just getting word, the mystery candidate is entering the debate stage now, and it's… Holy Cow, I can't believe it! *(FRANK and his NEWSGIRLS enter.)*

GLINDA: Frank Stein! He's the Dark horse candidate?

OMELAS: Now I know why he's not moderating the debate…

FRANK: Hello, everybody! Hello, Joe! It's good to see you!

COFFIN: Yeah, nice to see you too. And it'll be even nicer to see you lose!

NEWSGIRL 1: Don't listen to him, Frank! You're better than him on everything that counts!

NEWSGIRL 2: Yeah, yeah, hit him where it hurts!

NEWSGIRL 1: You beat him on the issues, you beat him on politics…

NEWSGIRL 2: Beat him like an egg! Scramble him!

FRANK: Don't worry, girls. I'll do my best. That's all anybody can do.

DOPPELGANGER: Oh, we're in trouble now.

MITSY: We're in trouble? Are you kidding? Frank Stein's a saint compared to Coffin Joe!

DOPPELGANGER: Exactly! He's not just good! He's too good!

PRODUCTION ASSISTANTS. *(Enter)*: Quiet on the set! You're live in five, four, three, two…

OMELAS: The rules are simple. The candidates will have opening statements, then answer questions with rebuttal. By a coin toss, the first up will be Mr. Frank Stein.

FRANK: Thank you, Omelas. And thanks to all of you watching this debate. This isn't just a news program you're watching right now. You're taking part in the adventure of American democracy!

MITSY: Oh no! You're right! He's… a nerd!

OMELAS: Thank you, Mr. Stein. Mr. Coffin, you're next.

COFFIN: Yeah, whatever. Look, I'm District Reaper! I got power! Big time power! Vote for me, or else! Capische?

MADDIE: He sounds like a bully.

MITSY: Well, that's why they call it the bully pulpit...

OMELAS: Okay. Mr. Stein, first question goes to you. What do you think should be done for the environment?

FRANK: We have to stop allowing big corporations to pollute our world. The ice caps are melting, the rainforests are vanishing. The bees are disappearing!

OMELAS: Thank you, Mr. Stein. Coffin Joe, a rebuttal?

COFFIN: The environment can kiss my rebuttal! We can't let hippies stand in the way of money! And since when do we care about bees? I don't like bees! Bees sting! You know what I say? No more bees! No more bees! No more bees! *(The crowd starts chanting "No more bees!"* MITSY *shakes her head.)*

OMELAS: Mr. Coffin, the next question is yours. Since you're so new to politics, do you really think you have the experience necessary for President?

COFFIN: Let me tell you about experience. I got plenty of it! I was at the firm of Screwtape & Associates for years and years! Why, I have as much experience as Doctor Frankenstein had when he made that chump over there! *(The crowd gasps.)*

OMELAS: Mr. Stein, a rebuttal?

FRANK: *(Takes off his glasses, and looks thoughtfully at* COFFIN JOE.) Mister Coffin, I knew Dr. Frankenstein. I worked with Dr. Frankenstein. Dr. Frankenstein was a friend of mine. Mister Coffin, you're no Dr. Frankenstein.

DOPPELGANGER: Good, good! Stein's not taking his bait! He's standing up to him! This could work!

COFFIN: Yeah, yeah. I'm glad I'm not Dr. Frankenstein. After all, he was a grave robber, a mad scientist...

FRANK: I'm not going to dignify that with a response...

COFFIN: And he was a deadbeat dad, too!

FRANK: *(Angry.)* You take that back you son of a witch! *(**FRANK** lunges at **COFFIN** but the **NEWSGIRLS** hold him back.)*

NEWSGIRL 1: Steady, Frank, steady! Don't let him get you mad!

NEWSGIRL 2: Yeah, mad's no good! Voters don't like mad!

FRANK: I don't care! Nobody insults my family and gets away with it!

NEWSGIRL 1: C'mon, Frank! You can't let him get you riled up like that!

NEWSGIRL 2: Yeah, you gotta stay calm! Relaxed! Cool under fire!

FRANK: *(Appears to begin a mental breakdown.)* Fire? Fire? Fire hurts! Fire bad! Bad! *(**FRANK** lumbers offstage with his hands up.)*

NEWSGIRL 1: You just had to go and say the "F" word in front of him, didn't you?

NEWSGIRL 2: Hey, don't blame me! You were the one who said we didn't need to prep him on Dr. Frankenstein!

NEWSGIRL 1: I know, I know!

NEWSGIRL 2: I kept saying, "Coffin Joe will bring it up in the debate!" And you kept saying, "No, he won't! He doesn't even know how to pronounce it!"

NEWSGIRL 1: Okay, you were right! Put it on your resume, why don't you?

NEWSGIRL 2: After this, I'll put it on my tombstone! *(They exit.)*

PRODUCTION ASSISTANTS: And we're out! *(**FRANK** is pulled away. **COFFIN** smiles.)*

COFFIN: I'm having fun!

DOPPELGANGER: No, no! This is terrible! Frank fell for the oldest trick in the book! He went full Frankenstein! They're probably bringing torches and pitchforks into the voting booth as we speak!

MADDIE: Ugh. I'd sell my soul for this election to just make sense...

MITSY: Ah! That's it! I've got it! I think I know how to solve this whole thing once and for all!

ARI and **DOPPELGANGER:** What? You do? *(Looking at each other.)* You're doing it again!

MITSY: Of course! It was staring me in the face all along! The soul trafficking, the afterlife deals, everything! I just gotta make a quick phone call! *(MITSY goes offstage with the phone.)*

OMELAS: Okay everybody, this just in. Frank Stein had to be sedated; therefore, the debate has been cut off and polling places are now open. *(Looks at his watch.)* Aaaaaand they're closed!

MADDIE: What! Already?

ARI: At least it's longer than they let people vote in the South.

OMELAS: We're just getting the numbers… Popular vote is in, 98 percent for Frank Stein, 2 percent for Coffin Joe! And the electoral college… 250 votes for Coffin Joe, 78 for Frank Stein.

MADDIE: But that doesn't make sense!

DOPPELGANGER: Of course it doesn't make sense! It's the electoral college!

OMELAS: That means with a margin of 172 votes, Coffin Joe is our new President! *(COFFIN hogs the microphone.)*

COFFIN: To all my supporters, thank you very much for all your help! And to everybody who voted for my opponent… I will hunt you down like dogs! From now on, I am the law! And there's nothing you can do to stop me!

MITSY: *(Enters dramatically.)* Not if I have anything to say about it!

MADDIE: Mitsy?

LUPINA: Mitsy, it's too late. He won!

MITSY: Oh, no he didn't. I just made a phone call with an important client. I had to pull a few strings, but he's gonna set everything straight!

COFFIN: Oh yeah? Dream on, sister! I've been wheeling and dealing for ages, and you'll never be able to beat me! You better give the devil his due…

DEVIL: *(Hopping onstage.)* The Devil, you say?

OMELAS: Okay, I have no idea what's going on anymore, but we're gonna kill in the ratings!

DEVIL: That's right; it's me! The Prince of Darkness! The Lord of the Flies! Beelzebub, Mr. Scratch, Good Ol' You-Know-Who!

COFFIN: I... Uh... I don't know what you're talking about!

MITSY: Sure, you do! You said you worked at Screwtape & Associates. I did business with them! But they never had anybody named "Coffin Joe"...

COFFIN: Well c'mon... "Coffin Joe" is just a political nickname! Of course they don't have anybody on the books with that name!

MITSY: Yes, that's true. But they did have someone named Jack Flash!

DEVIL: Yes, Jumping Jack Flash! One of my best devil's advocates... Until he turned his back and started working for the other side!

COFFIN: What are you talking about? I sent you all kinds of souls!

DEVIL: Yeah, you let bad guys go to heaven and sent good guys to me! They're no fun! I wanted to torture the souls of big businessmen, dictators, movie executives! People who really get their hands dirty! People like... well, you!

COFFIN: What are you talking about?

MITSY: *(Takes out a contract.)* This is the contract you signed with the Devil when you started your campaign to run for office! Read the fine print, Jackie boy!

COFFIN: In English, please?

DEVIL: It means you're coming with me!

COFFIN: Wait, wait! You can't do this! It's not fair!

DEVIL: Oh, come on now, Jackie boy! You should've known if you make a deal with the Devil, you're gonna get burned!

OMELAS: Hold on! If Coffin Joe's being taken away, then who's President?

DEVIL: Why, I am, of course!

MADDIE: He is?

MITSY: That's what the contract says!

DEVIL: That's right! *(Clears throat.)* I'll be issuing a statement later tonight. Rest assured, I intend to make this a kinder, gentler country for everyone!

DOPPELGANGER: Well, at least he's the lesser of two evils.

COFFIN: *(To MITSY.)* Please, Mitsy! You gotta get me out of this!

MITSY: Sorry, Joe. Or should I say, Jack. It's out of my hands!

COFFIN: But what am I supposed to do now?

MITSY: You know what you can do? *(The song "Hit the road, Jack" begins playing.)*

About the Author & Illustrator

Bob Clark is a writer, cartoonist, and storyboard artist from Westchester County, NY. He has written plays for children for over 20 years that have been performed in the Theatre in a Trunk programs in Albert Leonard Middle School and other after school and summer venues. *Mitsy Morte: Afterlife Attorney* is his first published work. He is also available for scriptwriting and story art for animation. His work can be found online at linktr.ee/neowestchester.